*So what ha...*

*a...*

Daniel wondered as he led the girl out onto the dance floor. He couldn't help but be impressed by her towering dignity. He hadn't heard what had been said, but he could guess that she'd been threatened. Nothing could be more demure than her demeanor now.

Not that this girl was any dewy innocent, he reminded himself dryly—not working in a place like this. But even so, there was more to this than met the eye.

On the crowded dance floor, she was crushed against him. He let his hand slip down over the base of her spine, holding her close as she tried to pull away from him, and was amused by the sudden flush of pink that colored her cheeks.

Of course, she could be just a damned good actress....

**SUSANNE McCARTHY** has spent most of her life in London, but after her marriage, she and her husband moved to Shropshire. The author is now an enthusiastic advocate of this unspoiled part of England, and although she has set her novels in other locations, Susanne says that the English countryside may feature in many of her books.

## Books by Susanne McCarthy

# SUSANNE McCARTHY

## Dance for a Stranger

## Harlequin Books

TORONTO • NEW YORK • LONDON
AMSTERDAM • PARIS • SYDNEY • HAMBURG
STOCKHOLM • ATHENS • TOKYO • MILAN
MADRID • WARSAW • BUDAPEST • AUCKLAND

Harlequin Presents first edition September 1992
ISBN 0-373-11493-1

Original hardcover edition published in 1991
by Mills & Boon Limited

DANCE FOR A STRANGER

# CHAPTER ONE

'But, my friend, I insist! You cannot leave Kahyanga without visiting the Paradise. The best whisky, the best girls... Ah, truly paradise!'

The tall, dark-haired Englishman regarded the seedy-looking night-club with a certain amount of distaste. It wasn't the sort of place he would have chosen to enter, but, after a long, weary day spent inspecting an open-cast bauxite mine in the sweltering tropical heat of the South China Sea, he could do with a drink.

The place was dimly lit, which was probably just as well. The air was thick with the smell of cheap alcohol and cigarette smoke. One of the 'best girls' Lee Chuan had promised was dancing in a cage above the bar, clad in a feather costume that didn't leave a great deal to the imagination. She looked bored stiff.

Lee Chuan nudged him, his narrow black eyes glittering like jets. 'The best, eh?' he gloated, watching the girl as if he had never seen a pair of legs before.

Daniel cast a cynical eye around the room. It was little more than a dive, popular with local businessmen eager to throw their money away on overpriced drinks and the company of one of the cheap-glamour 'hostesses' who served the place.

'What will it be, my friend?' Lee Chuan enquired genially. 'A whisky?'

Daniel nodded. It would probably taste like turpentine, but at the moment he would drink whatever was put in front of him. Still, his business had been settled to admirable satisfaction, and so tomorrow he could catch the plane back to Singapore, and then home.

Leaning back against the bar, his eye was suddenly caught by an altercation taking place along at the far end. One of the girls was having a row with the boss. She was standing up to him well, too, shaking her head and making an angry gesture with her hand, not in the least bit intimidated by the fact that he was all of six feet six and built like a brick wall.

He watched with interest. The big bully was making his point with a thick finger on the bar, and to Daniel's disappointment he seemed to be winning the argument. The girl shrugged her slim shoulders, still defiant, but she turned away, and the boss grinned with satisfaction, adjusting his slick bow-tie as he sauntered off across the cramped space that served as a dance-floor.

The girl had turned to lean on the bar, and now Daniel could see her face. She was quite a looker—big grey eyes with long silky lashes, skin as smooth as cream, and thick red-brown hair that fell straight and glossy to her shoulders. But it was her mouth that held the fatal fascination—wide and sensual, just made to be kissed. And there was a tiny brown mole just above the corner.

She seemed to sense that she was being watched, and glanced along the bar. Daniel let her read his approval, but she wasn't impressed. The sheer hostility in her glare surprised him a little. No wonder the boss had been lecturing her—that was no way to treat the paying customers.

Beside him, Lee Chuan was chuckling. 'You like that one, eh?' he enquired gleefully. 'I'll get them to send her to our table—and I'll take that sassy-looking blonde standing next to her.'

Daniel hesitated. Usually he had no time for those sort of girls, but he found himself mildly intrigued. Somehow she didn't look like the kind of girl he'd have expected to find working in a dump like this. Lee Chuan had already called the barman over, and was pointing out the girls he wanted. Daniel glanced around for an empty table.

'Good, eh?' Lee Chuan demanded, taking a seat and looking round to make sure the barman sent the right pair. 'I told you, the best girls in the whole of Kahyangan.' He rubbed his hands together in anticipation. 'We'll have a good time tonight, hm?'

She was coming over. Daniel leaned back in his seat, watching the way she moved. She was long and slender, just the way he liked them, and she walked with the easy grace of a dancer. Her dress was cheap and tacky—vivid blue satin, spangled with sequins, it was cut breathtakingly low at the front, with just thin straps over her shoulders, and the skirt was short enough to start a riot. But it wouldn't have mattered if she'd been wearing a potato sack—she'd have turned heads anywhere.

What a pity she was what she was. He had nothing but contempt for the type of man who would even consider paying for a woman, and he had no intention of setting aside the principles of a lifetime tonight—even though he had to admit that it would be almost worth it to find out if that luscious mouth and tempting body could deliver all they promised.

'Oh, come on, Rae. All we've got to do is sit with them for a bit and get them to buy us drinks. What's wrong with that?'

Rae slanted her friend a look of wry cynicism. 'That'd be fine,' she conceded. 'But do you really think that's all it's going to lead to?'

Mel giggled. 'Of course it will,' she asserted with confidence. 'When did either of us ever have the least trouble when it comes to handling men?'

'Yes, back in London,' Rae pointed out drily. 'But we're thousands of miles from London now. And you can see what sort of place this is.'

'Oh, don't be silly—it's a bit of a dump, but with a lick of paint and a few coloured spotlights it'd be all right. Besides, until we can get hold of Mr Nyein and get all this business about our contract sorted out, we've got to work. And anyway, they look nice—especially the tall one. Do you suppose they speak English?'

Rae hesitated for a moment, and then reluctantly gave in. For tonight, at least, she didn't have much choice. The gorilla who ran the place had made it quite clear that if any of them made trouble for him he would make trouble for them.

And they were in enough trouble already, it seemed. Mr Nyein, who had hired the five of them in London on a six-month contract to appear as cabaret dancers in a top-class night-club in Singapore, hadn't sorted out their work permits properly, so the club had refused to take them. After a good deal of hassle, Mr Nyein had managed to get them a temporary booking on Kahyangan, one of the hundreds of tropical islands floating on the hot blue of the South China Sea.

Rae had thought it a little suspicious at the time, but they had all been tired after the fifteen-hour flight from London, and confused by jet lag. And besides, none of them had the money to pay for their air-fare home. And so she had let herself be persuaded—against her better judgement—to fly on here with the others.

It had been dark when they had arrived, so they hadn't been able to see much of the place. All they had wanted to do was sleep. The attic they had been taken to hadn't been exactly luxurious, but then they hadn't expected much—cabaret dancers were rarely provided with decent accommodation. At least the beds were clean.

But this morning they had woken to find that Nyein had gone—back to Singapore, apparently, to sort out the problem with the night-club there, having handed their passports over to the big gorilla who ran this place, 'for registration purposes'. And when they had asked about rehearsal times the gorilla had simply laughed.

It had soon become all too clear what sort of club this was—it had taken only one look at the dresses they had been given to wear. But when they had protested, the gorilla had turned nasty. It had already cost him a great deal of money to fly them from Singapore, he had claimed angrily, and, until Nyein returned for them, if they didn't work, they didn't eat.

She glanced up at Angie, stuck up there in that cage above the bar in that awful skimpy costume. The gorilla had tried to make her go in there herself, but she'd refused. Poor Angie hadn't had the courage to argue with him. She'd been in there for over an hour now, dancing like a automaton, gazing at some point on the ceiling so she wouldn't have to see all the men ogling at her. And Liz was already having to dance with some fat old goat who smelled of sickly aftershave, helplessly signalling distress with her eyes as he pawed at her.

Well, so now it was her turn. The two businessmen who had bought their company were waiting. A wave of revulsion rose inside her. Men like that—they were beneath contempt. Tomorrow, come hell or high water, she was going to find a way to get out of this place, and get to the British Embassy. But first there was tonight to get through. Tilting her head at a haughty angle, she followed Mel across the room.

One of the men rose to his feet as they approached, offering them seats with a gallantry so patently false that it made Rae's lip curl in something very close to a sneer. 'Good evening, ladies,' he greeted them, his glittering eyes devouring them both. 'Thank you for joining us. Won't you have a drink?'

Mel sat down, flirting her eyelashes at him. 'Thank you. We'll have champagne,' she requested, as they had been instructed.

He chuckled knowingly. 'Of course, of course.' He put up his hand, snapping his fingers loudly to summon a waiter.

Rae accepted the other seat, and flickered a cool glance towards the second man. Mel had been right—he was good-looking. Too good-looking to need to come to a place like this to find his women, she reflected acidly. His hair was dark, with just a hint of curl, and the dim lighting of the club sculpted the hard, aquiline bones of his face with shadow. He was wearing a lightweight cream-coloured suit, of unmistakable quality, well cut to mould an impressive breadth of shoulder. And that air of arrogant self-assurance bespoke a man of power, a man who was accustomed to getting what he wanted.

And what he wanted at the moment, to judge from the insolent way he was surveying her body, was something that wasn't on the market, at any price. He noted her frosty glare with a slight sardonic smile, and said something to his companion in a language she didn't understand; she guessed it was the version of Indo-Chinese spoken here on the island—he seemed to speak it as fluently as a native, though his features defined him as European.

The first man laughed. 'My friend would like to know your name,' he said to her.

'Rae,' she responded tersely, refusing to look at him again.

'And you?' he asked Mel, easing a little closer to her.

Mel giggled up at him. 'I'm Melissa—but you can call me Mel; everyone does,' she invited fetchingly.

Rae flashed her friend a warning glance. It was all very well to play games in the clubs at home, where she could walk out and get straight into a taxi back to their flat, but out here it was decidedly dangerous. Already the man had his arm along the back of her seat, moving his head so that he could gaze straight down into her cleavage.

'Melissa,' he murmured, his voice soft and seductive. 'A beautiful name—for a beautiful young lady. I am Lee, and my companion here is——'

The tall man cut him off with a word. He reached across the table, and took Rae's hand. 'Would you care to dance?' he enquired.

So he *was* English. Somehow that seemed to make it worse, that one of her own countrymen should be so ready to pay for the kind of woman he obviously thought she was. She returned him a frosty glare. 'I don't think I feel like it just at the moment, thank you,' she rapped, withdrawing her hand.

Rather to her surprise, he accepted the rebuff, though she had an uncomfortable feeling that he was just marking time. The waiter had brought over two bottles of the cheap sparkling wine that was sold under the champagne label at expensive champagne prices, and uncorked one with a flourish, spilling the sparkling foam into their glasses.

The one who had introduced himself as Lee picked up two of the glasses, handing one to Mel. 'To your very good health,' he toasted, encouraging her to drink. Mel tipped back her glass, draining half of it in one go. Rae sighed inwardly. Mel was always convinced that she could hold her alcohol, but she rarely could.

Rae ignored her own glass. The other man took his, and sipped it sparingly, still watching her. She turned him an aloof shoulder, but she was still aware of his disconcertingly steady gaze resting on her. It made her feel uncomfortable, as if she were half-naked—if only this dress were a little more decent!

Lee had his arm around Mel by now, laughing with her as if he had never enjoyed an evening so much in his life. He caught the glint of scorn in Rae's eyes, and chuckled in mocking amusement. 'Hey, little lady, what's wrong?' he jeered. 'How about a smile?' Rae sat like a block of wood, rage and humiliation burning inside her. He leaned across the table, and pinched her cheek. 'Don't you like my friend?' he taunted. 'But he is much man, hm? Maybe he is too much man for you?'

That did it! That big stupid gorilla could threaten her as much as he liked—she wasn't going to stand for this a minute longer. With an abrupt movement she knocked his hand away, pushing her chair back from the table and rising to her feet. The tall man rose too, and she turned on him in vicious anger.

'*Leave* me alone,' she spat, so fiercely that he stepped back, his eyebrows raised in surprise. As Mel gaped, open-mouthed, she spun on her heel and stalked away across the room, her head held high.

A cheap beaded curtain hung across the door, and beyond was a kind of lobby. On one side was the flight of stairs that climbed up past several floors to the attic dormitory where they had been taken on their arrival; on the other was a dark narrow corridor, and the door out to the street.

Just for a second, her footsteps hesitated. There were two of the gorilla's henchmen at the door, and even if she could get past them it was dark outside and she had no idea of the way to the British Embassy. But as she was considering whether it might be better to retreat upstairs for now, the gorilla stepped through the curtain behind her.

'Where you think you go?' he demanded, his voice an unpleasant sneer. 'Get back inside—you here to work.'

She turned on him with a snarl. 'Work? That's not the kind of work I came here to do,' she threw at him furiously. 'I'm a dancer.'

'Sure.' He smiled, menacing her as he loomed over her. 'That what you here to do. Dance with customers. Be nice to them.'

A cold chill of fear gripped her heart. 'How nice?' she enquired cautiously.

He leered down at her. 'As nice as they want you to be,' he purred with evil relish. 'And if maybe they like you little bit...?' He lifted a strand of her long hair, and stroked it between his pudgy fingers. 'We got rooms upstairs you can be private. Very nice. You make a little more money.'

'Oh, no.' She shook her head. 'No—I'm leaving, right now. I'm going straight to the British Embassy.'

He laughed nastily, and suddenly she realised that the two other men had come up close behind her. 'You not go nowhere,' the gorilla growled. 'Not British Embassy, not police. They not help you— throw you in prison for owe money, break contract. You very silly girl.'

Before she had time to realise what was going to happen, a thick arm had grabbed her from behind, holding her round the waist so that it was hard to struggle, and a large palm covered her mouth, stifling her scream. As she put up her hand to defend herself, the gorilla grasped it, and covered her fist with his own great big one. And began to squeeze.

Tears of pain sprang to her eyes—if he went on squeezing like that, her bones would start to break. Staring up into his ruthless face, she knew he meant business. He wasn't afraid of any law. They were trapped, prisoners in this evil place.

He let her go abruptly, and she sank against the wall, cradling her injured hand gingerly. 'See? Now get back in there, earn your keep,' the gorilla ordered, shoving her back towards the door of the club. 'This last warning—next time I really hurt you.'

She turned to face him, tossing her hair in a last pathetic show of defiance. 'All right,' she retorted bitterly. 'I'm going.'

She felt sick as she walked back into the club. She couldn't have the least illusion about what they were really here for—and it certainly wasn't dancing. She had to find a way to get out—but how? They would be watching her even more closely now—it wasn't going to be easy to escape.

The man with the arrogant eyes was waiting for her. She met his cool gaze defiantly, determined not to betray the fear that was twisting inside her. He had bought her company—what was he going to expect for his money?

He held out his hand, faultlessly polite. 'Would you care to dance?'

She nodded, unable to speak, and allowed him to lead her out on to the crowded dance-floor.

So what had that been all about? Daniel mused to himself as he took her passive body into his arms. He couldn't help but be impressed by that towering dignity as she had scorned Lee Chuan's crude tormenting—she had been quite magnificent.

He hadn't liked it when he had seen that big thug who ran the place go out after her—though he was wryly aware that the instinct of chivalry that had made him follow had been, under the circumstances, rather foolhardy. He wasn't about to get his head kicked in for the sake of some cheap bargirl.

He hadn't heard what had been said, but he could guess that she had been threatened. Nothing could be more demure than her demeanour now—she had fixed her gaze somewhere on the open neck of his shirt, her long dark lashes shadowing her cheeks. He could almost imagine that he was dancing with one of the dewy young debs his mother was so fond of producing for him; heaven knew where she found them all—sometimes he suspected that she had a cupboardful hidden away somewhere.

Not that this girl was any dewy innocent, he reminded himself drily—not working in a place like this. But, even so, there was more to this than met the eye. She had stalked from the room like an outraged duchess, but a moment later she had been back, and that had unmistakably been fear in her eyes. The voice of common sense warned caution, but his curiosity was aroused. It would be very interesting to know what was going on here.

On the crowded dance-floor she was crushed against him, but he had no objection to that—her body was soft and slender, and her hair smelled of lemons and spice. He let his hand slip down to mould over the base of her spine, holding her close as she tried to pull away from him, amused by the sudden flush of pink that coloured her cheeks.

Of course, she could be just a damned good actress; this could all be part of her stock-in-trade—a little performance designed to part a fool from as much of his money as possible. He had no intention of sticking his neck out too far, but maybe he'd just play along with her for a while, and see if he could get to the bottom of this little mystery.

Rae felt as if she were shivering, though the air-conditioning in the club was having little effect on the sauna-heat of the tropical night. This man, with his strong arms, and his sardonic smile—she hated him, hated his touch. But deep inside her a strange kind of sensation had begun to stir. Maybe it was because she was so much in his power—or maybe it had something to do with the fascination of those few dark hairs that curled at the base of his throat, or the musky, masculine smell of his skin...

She stiffened, trying to hold herself away from him. She wasn't responding to him—he had no right to hold her so intimately close. She flashed him a look of icy disdain, but he merely laughed softly.

'So tell me,' he asked smoothly. 'What's a nice girl like you doing in a place like this?'

She glared at him, not appreciating the inflection of mocking humour in his voice. 'I work here,' she countered acidly.

'Have you been here long?'

'What's it to you?'

He shrugged his wide shoulders in a gesture of elegant indifference. 'Oh, merely making pleasant conversation,' he drawled, stroking his hand over the soft curve of her *derrière* in the clinging satin sheath, as if to emphasise that conversation was the last thing on his mind.

She felt herself tense in anger. But there was nothing she could do to retaliate—he had bought her for the evening, and that entitled him to say whatever he liked to her. And if she objected the consequences could be more than a little unpleasant.

Covertly she studied him from beneath her lashes. He was as handsome as the devil, with the sort of deep dark eyes that you could want to drown in. But there was an unmistakable hint of ruthlessness in the hard lines of his jaw. A tremor of primeval fear ran through her as she sensed a natural predator. And she was trapped. What if he decided that he wanted to take her upstairs?

But maybe... Was she being irrational? It could be that her fear of the gorilla and his threats were blurring her judgement. Perhaps this man could be quite reasonable. Did she dare tell him what had happened, beg him to take a message to the British Embassy?

Unconsciously she drew her bottom lip between her teeth, gnawing it as she tried to weigh up the odds. She really had no reason to trust him. After all, she knew nothing about him except that he had come into this club—and that was hardly any recommendation of good character. For all she knew, he could be a regular customer, even a friend of the gorilla—and if he should warn him of what she was trying to do...

Across the room she could see the gorilla watching her, a faint smile of satisfaction on his face. He clearly believed his bullying tactics had worked. Somehow she had to find a way of convincing him of that, so that he would relax his guard...

The audacity of her own plan almost took her breath away. Did she have the nerve to carry it off? If she failed, it could make things ten times worse. But there was no way she was going to give in and do as they wanted. They'd have to kill her first.

'Are you always this hostile with your customers, or is it just me?' her partner enquired conversationally.

Rae caught herself up swiftly, slipping into the role she would need to play. 'I'm sorry,' she purred, sweeping him a doe-eyed look from beneath her lashes. 'I didn't mean to be bad-tempered. It's just...so stifling hot in here.'

The darkening glint in his eyes warned her that her act was having the desired effect. 'It certainly is,' he murmured, the low, husky note of his voice smouldering layers of extra meaning into his words.

She laughed, soft and velvet, and let her body warm in his arms. He drew her even closer against him, and boldly she let her hand stray up to the nape of his neck, the pad of her thumb deliberately caressing the small hollow behind his ear. An unmistakable tremor of response ran through him, and she hid a small smile of triumph.

He danced well, with an easy sense of rhythm, and she couldn't help but be aware of the hard muscular strength of his body, so close to hers. The music was taped; whoever had recorded it had a taste for the sweepingly romantic—Lionel Richie, Roberta Flack...some of her favourites. The power of the emotions they expressed tugged at her dancer's instincts, and the sensuous sway of her body answered involuntarily. She let him mould her to him, closing her eyes, acting her part. It was really quite easy...

Hey, come on, she reminded herself sharply. Don't get carried away with this. You're supposed to be working up to stage two of your escape plan.

But what did she do next? Wait for him to suggest that they went upstairs? But she couldn't be sure that that was what he was intending—he might just be content to dance with her. Maybe she should just drop him a little hint?

Leaning up on tiptoe, she put her mouth close to his ear. 'Don't you think it's a little crowded in here?' she whispered softly. 'We can't really...get to know each other properly.'

She felt him stiffen—had she been too clumsy? 'That's very true,' he agreed, a sardonic inflexion in his voice. 'What do you have in mind?'

'Just that...maybe we could find somewhere a little more...private?' She cast an anxious glance across the room at the gorilla. Was he going to fall for this? Slanting her companion another seductive

look, she let a small provocative smile play around
her lips, an invitation that no one could misread.

He laughed—but it was a harsh, mocking laugh.
'All right,' he conceded, a hard edge in his voice.
'How much do you charge?'

A scarlet blush coloured her cheeks. She should
have expected such humiliation—but she had to go
through with it. 'I . . .' How much should she say?

'Or should I discuss that with the boss, rather
than you?'

'Oh . . . yes, of course,' she agreed quickly; that
was probably how it worked—they wouldn't allow
the girls to take the money themselves.

'Then what are we waiting for?' He took her
hand in a firm clasp—it felt like a vice—and drew
her over towards the bead curtain. As they passed
their table—empty now, as Mel was dancing with
the other man—he picked up the second bottle of
champagne. Rae smiled grimly to herself. She had
been hoping he would do that—at least she knew
she would have something to hit him over the head
with.

A few of the men at the bar surveyed her with
lewd interest as they passed. She held herself very
erect, trying to look neither to right nor left. If the
other girls saw what she was doing, they might well
give the game away.

The gorilla was standing by the door. He cast her
a glance of mocking contempt, and she lowered her
eyes, trying to look convincingly defeated. She
heard a brief negotiation, and saw money ex-

changed for a key, and then he stood aside to let them pass.

'Excellent! Enjoy yourselves, hm?' He chuckled with such gloating satisfaction that Rae felt her hand clench in anger. With a bit of luck he would be laughing on the other side of his face before many more minutes had passed!

The stairs led up to a long dark corridor, lined with narrow hotel-room doors. The stranger stopped before one of them, and slipped the key in the lock. Rae waited, her mouth dry, her heart pounding so hard she was afraid he could hear it. Maybe this hadn't been such a good idea after all—but it was far too late to think of another plan now.

He held the door open for her, and she found herself stepping into a dark, exotic bedroom, heavily draped with red hangings—covering the windows, surrounding the bed. And there were mirrors in rich gilded frames—even one on the ceiling.

Behind her he laughed softly. 'Brothel chic,' he remarked, a lilt of sardonic amusement in his voice. With one hand on the small of her back he propelled her into the room, and she heard the door close behind them, heard the key turn in the lock again. 'So—no doubt you'll be expecting me to offer you a little for yourself, by way of...a tip?' he suggested, not troubling to hide the contempt in his voice. She turned to stare at him, unable to speak. He drew out his wallet. 'Shall we say fifty rupals?' He peeled off several notes. 'That's for the whole night.'

She bit her lip, watching as he laid the money down on the bedside table, and slipped his wallet back into his pocket. He had put the champagne bottle down on that table too, and she couldn't get at it without getting past him. And she couldn't see anything else heavy enough to knock him out with.

He was coming towards her, but she couldn't back away—those dark, mesmerising eyes seemed to be holding her captive. He came very close to her, and let his gaze drift down over the curves of her body in a way that sent a shimmer of heat down her spine. Her mind had gone blank—what was it she had planned to do next?

Very slowly he lifted one hand, sliding his fingers through her hair to cage her skull. She stared at him, scarcely able to breathe. His head bent over hers, and she felt the warmth of his breath on her cheek. 'Fifty rupals is a lot of money,' he murmured, the low, husky note of his voice caressing her. 'But somehow I think you're going to be worth every cent.'

The hot tip of his tongue lapped sensuously along her lips, parting them slightly, and then his teeth took hold of the soft fullness of her lower lip, nibbling at it gently, erotically. A betraying tremor of response ran through her. No one had ever kissed her like this before.

He drew her close against him, wrapping his arms around her, and she felt herself melting, unable to fight the tide of weakness that was flooding through her. As his mouth claimed hers she could only surrender, all the reasons why they were here together in this opulent bedroom forgotten.

Her body was curved tightly against the hard length of his, and the caressing touch of his hand burned her soft skin through the cheap slippery fabric of her dress. The intimate way he held her, and the plundering demand of his kiss, warned of a fierce male arousal that expected satisfaction.

But some corner of her mind still retained a shred of sanity. This was the moment—if she could just reach that champagne bottle... He growled in pleasure as she moved against him, unaware that she was stretching out her hand behind his back until...just, her fingers could curl around the neck of the bottle.

He lifted his head, his dark eyes glinting with mocking approval. 'Mmm—more than worth it,' he taunted softly. 'But I don't think——'

The blow caught him sharply on the back of the head, and he crumpled into her arms.

# CHAPTER TWO

GOODNESS, he was heavy—much heavier than Rae had anticipated. It was all she could do to lay him down safely on the bed. She stood watching him, anxiously biting her lip. He was all right, wasn't he? She hadn't killed him, anyway—he was still breathing—but his face looked rather grey. What if she had given him a serious concussion?

She bent over him, belatedly regretting what she had done. But as she touched his cheek he began to stir. Starting back quickly, she looked around for the best escape route. The window was the first possibility. She ran across the room and pulled aside the curtain. Damn—it was barred. She might have known.

Quickly she darted back to the bed. The key—he had put it in his pocket, but which one? Frantically she began to search through his jacket—she had only a few minutes until he came round, and then all hell would break loose. Maybe she should try to tie him up and gag him before she left...

Suddenly a hand caught at her wrist. She was so startled that she almost cried out. He was glaring up at her, his fingers tightening their grip like a vice. 'What the...?'

'Shh,' she pleaded urgently. 'Hush. Oh, please, I'm sorry I hit you.'

'Oh, was that what it was?' he drawled with biting sarcasm. 'I thought it was that dynamite kiss that had knocked me out.' He put his hand into the inside pocket of his jacket, and drew out his wallet.

'I haven't robbed you!' she protested in furious indignation.

'So it seems.' He put the wallet back, having satisfied himself of its contents. 'Obviously you didn't hit me hard enough.'

'Oh, please, I'm really sorry. Did I hurt you?' she asked anxiously.

'Only my pride,' he responded with cynical humour, rubbing his head. 'I never thought I'd be dumb enough to fall for that one.'

'You think I brought you up here just to steal your wallet?' she demanded, angry.

He lifted a sardonic eyebrow. 'Well, didn't you?' he countered mockingly.

'No, I didn't! I . . . I just had to find some way to get out of here.'

'Well, I must admit the décor isn't exactly to my taste either,' he conceded, eyeing the opulent splendour of the room with distaste. 'But was it really necessary to go to such lengths?'

'I'm serious,' she insisted impatiently. She studied him anxiously, chewing on her lower lip. Much as she hated being beholden to a man like this, she was going to have to take a chance and tell him the truth—but, after what she had done, could she make him believe her? Those dark eyes were watching her steadily, their cynical glint warning her that he was going to doubt every word. 'It...it's a long story.'

'Really?' he mocked. 'I'd be very interested to hear it.' With a polite gesture of his hand he invited her to sit down.

Warily she perched on the very end of the bed, as far away from him as possible, trying hard to hang on to some shreds of her dignity. 'You see, I'm a dancer,' she began diffidently.

'Ah!'

She slanted him a frosty glare. 'We were supposed to be going to Singapore,' she explained, refusing to let him needle her. 'We had a contract to appear at a night-club there—at least we thought we did. But there was some sort of mix-up, or so he said...'

He held up his hand to stay the garbled flow. 'Wait a minute,' he pleaded. 'Who said?'

'Mr Nyein—the man who auditioned us in London,' she backtracked impatiently. 'Anyway, he brought us here instead, though he didn't tell us what sort of a place it is,' she added with a shudder.

'I'm sure he didn't.'

'I'm telling you the truth!' she insisted, stung by his scepticism.

He lifted one sardonic eyebrow a fraction of an inch. 'Really? Are you sure you know what that is?'

Stupid tears sprang to her eyes. 'I hate you!' she spat. 'I wish I *had* hit you harder—I hope I really hurt you.'

'Well, you have that hope granted, at least,' he responded wryly. 'OK, so carry on—you'd got to the bit where Nyein had brought you here.'

She hesitated, wondering if it was worth wasting her breath. But he had the key, so he made the rules. 'Well, then he disappeared,' she continued. 'And the gorilla that runs the place had our passports, and he said we owed him a lot of money because he'd paid our air-fares and that we had to work for him, and if we didn't he threatened to lock us up in the attic without any food.'

'I see. Well, at the very least it seems that you and your friends have been remarkably naïve, getting yourselves conned into a situation like this.'

'I know,' she retorted, her eyes flashing. 'It's all very well for you to sit there being so condescending, but it really all seemed perfectly all right at the audition. Besides, it isn't very easy to get a job as a dancer, you know. You have to have an equity card, and you can't get one of those unless you've got a job.'

'Catch twenty-two.'

'This would have been just the experience we needed,' she sighed wistfully. 'It was a great chance.'

'That's what creeps like your Mr Nyein depend on—that you'll be so keen to come, that you won't notice the little flaws in the set-up.'

'But you do believe me?' she pleaded, her wide, anxious eyes on his face.

An enigmatic smile curved his hard mouth. 'I won't commit myself to that just yet,' he countered guardedly. 'I suppose it didn't occur to you to tell me all this *before* you hit me?'

'I didn't think you'd be interested in listening,' she countered with taut acerbity. 'After all...'

'That wasn't what I'd paid for?'

Her cheeks flamed a heated red, and he laughed softly, watching her with a speculative glint in his eyes as he reached out and picked up his fifty rupals from the bedside table and tucked it back into his wallet. 'Suppose for a moment that you *are* telling the truth,' he mused, 'just how far would you have been prepared to go with this little charade?'

'I...I wouldn't have...'

He watched as her blush deepened, and then laughed. 'No, maybe you wouldn't, at that,' he mused. 'I'm no expert on the subject, of course, but I wouldn't have expected a professional—er—hostess to blush and chew her lip the way you do.'

'I'm not a professional hostess,' she protested in hot indignation. 'I told you, I'm a dancer.'

'Are you?' He leaned over and put one hand beneath her chin to tilt up her face, and his eyes searched hers for a long moment, as if trying to plumb the very depths of her soul. 'I don't know,' he murmured. 'Maybe you're just a very clever little actress...'

That dark gaze was almost mesmerising, making her feel as though she were drowning. Her heart had begun to race far too fast, and she had to look away from him quickly to break the spell. 'Anyway, you seem to know an awful lot about professional hostesses,' she challenged acidly.

He laughed with dry humour. 'Not from first-hand experience, I assure you.'

'No?' All her wary suspiciousness was back in her eyes. 'Then why did you agree to come up here with me?'

'Maybe I was simply curious to find out what you were up to,' he responded, his face maddeningly difficult to read. 'Or maybe it was an offer I just couldn't refuse.'

She regarded him with wary suspicion. 'How do I know if I can trust you?' she queried cautiously.

'You don't,' he conceded with an indifferent shrug. 'But you're going to have to take a chance if you want to get out of here, aren't you?'

She regarded him thoughtfully for a moment. It was the very cynicism of his words that convinced her—if he had tried to persuade her with sweet arguments she would have simply closed her ears.

'Very well,' he concluded, a mocking smile curving that hard, sensual mouth. 'If we've agreed to give each other the benefit of the doubt, at least for now, the next thing to do is to find some way out of here.' He glanced around the room. 'Is the window any good?'

She shook her head. 'It's barred.'

'It would be. So it looks like the corridor, then. Is there a back way out?'

'I don't know.'

He drew the key from his pocket. 'We'd better have a look, then, hadn't we?' he suggested.

She hesitated, biting her lip again. 'You don't have to help me,' she reminded him tensely—though what she would do if he didn't she had no idea. 'It could be dangerous.'

His dark eyes glinted with self-mocking humour. 'At the moment, I'm inclined to think that you're a great deal more dangerous than that gorilla of yours,' he drawled. 'And I'm probably going to regret that I ever let myself get dragged into this. But since I have, let's get going, before anyone comes along.'

He moved quietly across the room—for such a big man, he was surprisingly light on his feet. Turning the key silently in the lock, he opened the door a fraction of an inch. The corridor was still empty. Reaching back, he took her hand, and drew her out after him.

Fear was knotting in her stomach, but the touch of his hand was strangely reassuring. She followed him down the corridor, tiptoeing, almost afraid to breathe. The corridor elbowed to the left, and there was another flight of stairs, steep and narrow and pitch dark.

'Careful,' he whispered close to her ear. 'I'll go first.'

One step at a time, they eased their way down, she clinging to his arm, afraid of falling. The increasingly pungent smell of cheap alcohol suggested they were coming to some kind of store-room behind the bar.

'Last step,' he whispered.

Gingerly she established that she was on level ground again, but then, putting out her hand, she touched, instead of the wall, a pile of wooden crates covered in soft cobwebs. Biting back the impulse to scream, she shook her hand quickly to brush off the creepy things.

'There's a window,' he whispered, leaning close to her ear and pointing to a dim square of grey high on the far wall.

She nodded. 'Can you get it open?'

'I can give it a try...'

Suddenly there was a noise, and as they both ducked instinctively to the stone floor another door opened. Light and music from the bar spilled into the store-room. Rae closed her eyes tightly, expecting at any moment a cry of discovery. If it hadn't been for his hand on her shoulder, protective and reassuring, she would have gone to pieces.

But the only sound was of tuneless humming, and a barrel being dragged across the floor. The door closed again, leaving them in the silent darkness. She heard him let go his breath in a silent whistle through his teeth. 'Phew—that was close.'

She laughed in relief as they stood up again. 'You know, I don't even know your name,' she whispered.

'Daniel Amory.' He held out his hand to her in formal politeness, and she shook it automatically. 'I'm very pleased to meet you,' he teased, his voice lilting with amusement at the incongruous introduction. 'Come on, let's get out of here.'

They crossed to the window. Rae regarded it dubiously. 'It's very small,' she whispered. 'I'll be able to get through it all right, but will you?'

'I'll manage. But it seems to be locked—we need something to prise it open. Find a crowbar or something.'

'A crowbar.' She nodded, and turned around. In the dark, she was going to have to search with her hands—and there were all those cobwebs. Suppressing a shudder, she began to feel along the piles of crates, trying not to think about spiders.

At last her fingers touched cold iron. She picked it up, feeling along its length. It seemed strong enough. Stepping carefully among the piles of crates, she took it back to him. 'Will this do?'

'That's fine.'

Carefully he eased the end of the crowbar into the frame of the window, just below the catch. As his powerful shoulders hunched with the effort, Rae held her breath, terrified that it would make a noise loud enough to alert the gorilla and his men. But with a creak it began to give way, swinging open on its hinges.

'Oh, thank goodness!' she breathed, closing her eyes for a brief second in relief.

'Come on,' urged Daniel quickly. 'I'll give you a leg-up.'

The window was level with her forehead, and nimble as she was she would never have been able to get out by herself. He bent and made a stirrup with his hands, and she put one foot in it, seeking with her hands for a place to grip the top of the window-frame and pull herself up backwards.

The store-room was a semi-basement, so the window was only just above ground level outside.

It was quite easy for her, once she was up, to perch
on the edge of the frame and ease out first one leg
and then the other. That she was giving Daniel a
generous display of her long, slender thighs did not
seem to matter, under the circumstances—it was no
time for foolish modesty.

'OK,' she whispered as soon as she was safely
out. 'Can you manage?'

'Yes—mind out of the way.'

With a surge he levered himself up, manoeuvring
his wide shoulders through the narrow gap—it was
a very tight squeeze. Briefly Rae reflected on how
very strong he must be to haul himself up like that
with only the power of his own arms. And then he
was standing beside her. 'Thank you.' It seemed so
inadequate, after what he had done. Impulsively
she leaned up, and kissed him on the mouth.

A flicker of fire lit his dark eyes, and he put his
arms around her, drawing her against him. 'My
pleasure,' he growled, his head bending over hers.

How could she refuse him? Her lips parted to
admit the sensuous exploration of his tongue, deep
into the innermost secret corners of her mouth,
stirring again that irresistible response. Her head
felt so dizzy that she had to wrap her arms around
his neck to keep herself from falling off the planet;
that evocative male muskiness of his skin was
drugging her senses.

At last he lifted his head, his unfathomable dark
eyes glinting with amusement. 'Very nice,' he murmured, an inflexion of sardonic humour in his
voice. 'But I think perhaps we'd better get a little

further away from here before you express any more of your gratitude.'

She drew back quickly out of his arms, biting her lip—incredibly, she had forgotten for a moment the danger they had just escaped. 'Oh...yes...of course,' she stammered, struggling to regather the threads of her sanity. 'Mel and the others are still in there—I have to find the British Embassy, and get some help.'

'Unfortunately there isn't an Embassy on Kahyangan—it's too small,' he informed her with a wry smile. 'These islands come under the aegis of the British High Commissioner in Singapore. There's merely an honorary consul, Sir George Havering.'

'Well, I'd better go and see him, then. Do you know where he lives?'

He nodded. 'We'll take a taxi. But don't expect too much of old George—I'm afraid he's more interested in his golf and his tropical fish than the welfare of Her Majesty's subjects abroad.'

'Oh.' She lifted wide, anxious eyes to his face. 'But what am I going to do? I have to get them out—heaven knows what might happen to them in there.'

He studied her in curious speculation for a moment, but then he smiled reassuringly, slipping a casual arm around her shoulders. 'Don't worry,' he promised, 'we'll get them out somehow. Come on.'

The window they had escaped from was in a dark alley behind the night-club. Tall, narrow buildings, all jumbled together, rose on each side of it, and it seemed to have become a dump for all kinds of unpleasant rubbish that Rae didn't care to examine too closely as they picked their way carefully along it.

The impact of the street almost took her breath away. Even though it was almost midnight, the road was choked with traffic—American cars covered with chrome, and battered old diesel trucks, and noisy mopeds piled dangerously high with deliveries, all snarling along nose-to-tail, ignoring the directions of the uniformed traffic police with their shrill whistles adding ineffectually to the din.

'Watch your step,' Daniel reminded her, taking her arm as he eased a path for her through the crowds.

It was a timely warning—the street sloped steeply downwards towards the old typhoon shelter in the harbour, and the colonnaded pavement in front of each shop was a step down from its neighbour. Besides, many shops were still open, their stocks displayed outside, and along the pavements were hawkers and stalls, and even one or two beggars sitting on the ground. And amid all this, wherever there was space, someone had set up tables and chairs, and was serving satays and dim sum and fried noodles, cooked over a flaming brazier right there in the street.

The night was as hot as a sauna, and the noise, the bright lights, and the rich cooking smells assailed all Rae's senses in a bewildering carousel. 'Does it stay like this all night?' she asked Daniel as she fended off yet another trader trying to persuade her to stop and look at the colourful batik-printed cotton dresses and fake designer-label T-shirts massed along the front of his stall.

'Oh, the shops will start to close around midnight,' he told her with a grin. 'Then the traffic starts to thin out a bit, though it's never really quiet.'

'Phew—what a place to live!'

He stepped to the kerb to hail one of the little open-backed three-wheeled taxis—as soon as he lifted his hand, several of them swerved into the kerb, their two-stroke engines puttering smokily. Rae regarded them with some misgiving—there was only a shiny wrought-chrome side-rail to protect the passengers from the rest of the traffic. But after some swift haggling Daniel had agreed a fare with one of the drivers, and turned to hand her into the back of one of them.

'Are they safe?' she enquired in apprehension. 'It looks like a milk float.'

'Don't worry,' he reassured her with a dry smile. 'They don't tip over very often.'

'Oh, thank you,' she murmured, settling herself on the plastic bench-seat across the back. 'That makes me feel very confident.'

It was an unforgettable ride. Every jolt threw her against Daniel's hard, muscular body, until he put a protective arm around her to hold her safe against him. Most of all she was grateful that he was continuing to help her—he really had no reason to, but she wasn't sure what she would have done without him, especially if the consul turned out to be as unhelpful as he had suggested.

It took about fifteen minutes to leave the teeming narrow streets of the old town behind; they turned on to a wide avenue, where the fast-paced construction of ultra-modern office blocks and shopping precincts was showing the island's determination to present at least the face of a booming economy. Here the traffic was moving more swiftly, and as the flimsy taxi accelerated Rae gripped the side-rail nervously, though the flow of air that stirred her hair was pleasantly cool.

They took a left at some traffic-lights, and soon they were climbing the zigzag road up the side of the high peak that overlooked the harbour and the town. Below them a carpet of lights spread down to the tranquil sea, and in the distance the dark, mysterious shapes of the outlying islands rose against the black velvet sky. There was no moon tonight, and few stars; up here the air was sweet with the perfume of frangipani, and the chirping song of the cicadas seemed like the very sound of silence.

'Mm—it's like heaven up here,' sighed Rae, drawing in a long, pure breath.

He laughed softly. 'And hell is below us,' he murmured, lacing his hand into her hair and idly letting the long silken strands run through his fingers. 'To which do you belong, I wonder?'

A flutter of nervous agitation caught at her heart. He was so very close . . . Surreptitiously she tried to pull at the hem of her skirt, conscious of the way it had ridden up as she sat down to reveal rather too much of her long legs. No wonder he found it so hard to believe that she was a respectable girl— this dress made her look like a tart.

The taxi jerked to a halt outside the gates of a large white colonial villa. A neatly clipped lawn, dotted with immaculately kept beds of azaleas and roses, fronted the building; lights blazed in several of the downstairs windows, and half a dozen expensive cars in the drive warned that the consul had guests.

Daniel paid the taxi-driver, and offered Rae his hand to help her down from the back. She hesitated, biting her lip. How could she go knocking on the door of such an elegant house dressed like this? 'Couldn't I . . . couldn't I wait here?' she suggested tentatively.

Daniel laughed. 'Now is hardly the moment to start acting coy,' he taunted. 'You have to see him yourself.' But he took her hand in an encouraging clasp. 'Come on—it'll be all right.'

'But he's got people there . . .'

Reluctantly she let him lead her up the gravel drive. His firm knock was answered by a lofty, stone-faced butler. He glanced at Daniel, clearly recognising him, and then permitted his gaze to wander over Rae with nicely refined disdain before returning to Daniel again. 'Good evening, sir,' he greeted him, stiffly polite.

'Good evening, Rogers. Is Sir George at home?'

With a rustle of silk taffeta evening gown, a tall, elegant woman moved swiftly across the hall. 'Why,

Daniel!' She held out both her hands to him coquettishly, reaching up to peck him on the cheek. 'How delightful! I didn't even know you were in Kahyangan.'

Rae, standing by, ignored, felt more uncomfortable than ever. The woman was in her middle years, though her fine skin was very well preserved; her thick ash-blonde hair was swept up in a regal style, and the diamonds at her throat were undoubtedly real. She must have been quite beautiful when she was younger.

'But don't stand out here,' she purred, drawing Daniel into the house. 'Come on in. You'll have a drink? We've finished dinner, of course, ages ago, but there are quite a few people still here.'

'Thank you, Margot,' he responded, an inflexion of dry humour in his voice. 'Unfortunately I'm not here to socialise. I need to see George.'

She pouted, for the first time allowing her eyes to flicker in Rae's direction. Just that brief glance was quite sufficient to convey her distaste. 'Oh, I might have known it was business,' she chided Daniel, her eyes flirting with him. 'Rogers, call Sir George. But I'm very cross with you,' she went on, linking her hands through Daniel's arm and turning her back on Rae with supreme upper-class rudeness. 'You know I always have my little dinners on Sundays. You should have let me know you were here.'

'And give you the problem of having a spare man?' he responded lightly. 'I wouldn't dream of putting you to such inconvenience.'

'Oh, you...!' She gave a tinkling laugh. 'George, look who's here,' she added as her husband appeared in the doorway. 'Isn't this nice?'

The gentleman appeared a good deal less than pleased. Rae guessed shrewdly that he was some years older than his wife. He was also about two inches shorter, with thin shoulders and receding hair that appeared once to have been ginger and was now nearly all grey. A precisely trimmed ginger-grey moustache added the only distinction to a pallid face, and his expensively tailored black dinner-jacket would have looked better left on its hanger.

'Amory,' he greeted his new guest with barely concealed dislike. 'What do you want?'

Daniel smiled drily, and, detaching himself from Lady Margot's clasp, he drew Rae forward. 'Perhaps we'd better go into your office?' he suggested.

The consul cast a disparaging glance over Rae. 'Very well,' he conceded grudgingly. 'This had better be important.' He stalked across the hall, and threw open another door. 'Come in.'

'Now don't go slipping away afterwards,' pleaded his wife, smiling up at Daniel with sparkling eyes. 'You must stay and have a drink with us—I simply insist.'

'We'll see,' was all Daniel would promise. He put his hand on Rae's arm, and guided her into Sir George's office.

It was an imposing room, panelled in gleaming oak, with a large portrait of the Queen, wearing the dark blue ribbon of the Order of the Garter, hanging on the wall behind the desk. Along the opposite wall stood several large, green-lit tanks of exotic tropical fish.

'Take a seat,' invited Sir George impatiently, strolling over to examine one of the tanks. 'You'd better tell me what this is all about, young lady. I've had to leave my guests, you know.' His baleful glare threatened her with the direst consequences if she should prove to be wasting his time.

She sat down in the low chair he indicated, trying again to tug her short skirt down a little. 'Well...' She bit her lip—this was all going to sound so foolish. But her anxiety for her friends made her bold, so, taking a deep breath, she began her story. The expression on his face as he listened to her was so disapproving that she felt her cheeks colouring with embarrassment.

Only when she mentioned the name of the nightclub did he look startled. 'The Paradise?' he repeated sharply.

'You know it?'

His eyes flickered with indignation. 'Of course I don't!' he snapped impatiently. 'What do you think I would be doing in a place like that? I know *of* it, however,' he conceded with haughty dignity. 'Not a particularly salubrious place, from what I hear.'

'It isn't,' she agreed, shuddering. 'Anyway, the man who owns it threatened us. He took away our passports, and he was holding us prisoner to make us work in the club as...as hostesses.'

'I see.' He moved across to sit in the large leather chair behind the desk, placing his elbows very precisely on the arm-rests and making a steeple with his bony fingers. 'And where exactly do you come into this, Amory?'

Rae slanted Daniel a look of apology. She had unwittingly placed him in a most embarrassing situation—he would surely not have wanted his friends to know about his visit to the Paradise. But he didn't seem to be the least bit troubled by Sir George's insinuations. 'I met Miss Dillon inside the club,' he explained, skirting neatly over the more awkward details. 'Naturally, when she told me her story, I did everything I could to help.'

'Most creditable,' approved the consul with an unpleasant smile. 'I wasn't aware that you favoured that sort of watering-hole. Or have they cleaned up their act since the last I heard of it?'

'That depends on what you last heard of it,' Daniel returned evenly, refusing to let himself be needled.

Sir George let his eyes drift over Rae's tacky attire. 'It doesn't seem to have changed a great deal,' he remarked, his insinuating tone making her wish she could sink through the floor. 'Well, why have you come to see me?'

'My friends are still in there,' she explained urgently.

He lifted his grey eyebrows a fraction of an inch. 'And what exactly do you expect me to do about it?' he enquired, as if she were slightly deranged.

'Well . . . help them get away, of course.'

'But from what you say you're all under a contract to work at this club,' he argued coolly. 'I really don't see that I can interfere.'

'Yes, we had a contract, but to work as dancers, not as...as...' She turned her eyes helplessly to Daniel, pleading with him to intervene.

'Perhaps you should telephone the police?' It was worded as a polite suggestion, but the note of quiet command in Daniel's voice lent it far more weight than that.

Sir George bridled in a show of indignation, but he couldn't meet Daniel's hard eyes. '*I'll* decide whether I should ring the police,' he blustered. 'Do you have any proof of what you say?' he demanded, turning back to Rae.

'Proof?' She stared at him blankly.

'You claim that you were being held prisoner. In that case, how do you come to be here?'

'Daniel...Mr Amory told you—he helped me to escape. We got out of a window.'

'Really?' There was a sharp edge of sarcasm in his tone. 'Well, Amory, how very chivalrous of you.'

Daniel laughed without humour. 'Wasn't it?' he agreed drily. 'And now it's your turn. Are you going to call the police?'

Sir George hesitated, but something in the grim line of Daniel's mouth warned him not to embark on a confrontation that would inevitably result in loss of face. 'Oh, very well,' he conceded at last. 'I'll do what I can.'

The conversation he conducted was in English—he seemed to think that if he wasn't understood he need only speak slower and louder, and his eyes signalled weary exasperation as if he thought Rae and Daniel would be in sympathy with him.

He was getting absolutely nowhere, and at last Daniel held out a peremptory hand for the telephone. Reluctantly Sir George passed it to him. Daniel spoke swiftly, in the island's own language. After a few moments he nodded, and put down the receiver. 'They'll meet us at the club in half an hour,' he announced. 'Rae, it'd be better if you stayed here.'

'Oh, no, I want to come——'

'Stay here,' he insisted firmly. 'I'm not sure that we can place much faith in the police—the local chief's likely to be on your gorilla's payroll.'

Her eyes widened. 'Oh, lord—do you really think so?' she breathed, horrified. 'You will be careful, won't you?'

He smiled with sardonic humour. 'Your concern is very touching,' he mocked. 'But don't worry, we won't have any trouble.'

Sir George sighed again. 'I just hope you're right,' he grumbled, rising to his feet. 'I suppose I'm going to have to come along too.' He was clearly annoyed about the whole thing. 'If you'll excuse me, I have to take my leave of my dinner-guests.' He stalked from the room, every inch the self-sacrificing public servant.

Rae looked up shyly at Daniel. It was impossible to tell what he was thinking—those dark eyes gave nothing away. He caught her watching him, and lifted one eyebrow in quizzical enquiry. 'It's...very good of you to go to all this trouble for me,' she murmured diffidently. 'I really don't know how to thank you.'

A dark flame flickered in the depths of his eyes. 'Oh, I dare say we'll be able to think of something,' he murmured smokily, drawing her to her feet and into his arms.

He was making it more than clear what he was expecting—that in return for his help she would go to bed with him. And she knew that she shouldn't give him any reason to believe that she would comply. But as his head bent over hers, and their mouths melted together, all common sense flew out of the window. She lifted her arms and wrapped them tightly around his neck, reaching up yearningly, holding nothing back as he plundered deep into the sweetest corners, claiming a possession that seemed to be his by right.

No man had ever kissed her the way he did. She closed her eyes, letting herself be swept away on a tide of honeyed warmth that filled her whole body, urging her to surrender. His hand had slid down to mould intimately over the base of her spine, curving her so close against him that she felt almost overwhelmed by the sheer masculine power of his body...

'Ahem.'

Rae broke from Daniel's arms, her cheeks flaming scarlet as she realised that Lady Havering was standing in the doorway, watching them. Those thin scarlet lips pursed into an expression of highly bred disdain, but she took Daniel's arm in a proprietorial clasp. 'Now you naughty boy!' she scolded archly, drawing him away from Rae's side. 'You were going to slip away, when you promised to stay and have a drink.'

'I'm sorry, Margot,' he responded, all easy charm. 'Another time, maybe? But Miss Dillon will be staying here while we're gone—take care of her for me, will you?'

'I see.' Eyes like diamond chips swept down over her, making not the slightest attempt to conceal what she was thinking. 'Well, Miss Dillon, perhaps you'd like a sherry?'

'Er—yes, please,' she stammered uncertainly. She had never in her life encountered someone as blatantly rude, and she had no idea how to deal with it.

'Stay here—I'll bring it to you.' Clearly she did not wish her guests to see her unwelcome visitor.

'Bitch,' muttered Rae under her breath as Lady Havering swept from the room.

Daniel laughed softly, and drew her into his arms. 'You can hardly blame her, my beguiling little witch,' he teased. 'Forgive me for saying so, but in that dress...'

Rae's eyes flashed in hot fury. 'I told you—I'm a professional dancer,' she protested, trying to break away from his embrace. 'If you still don't believe me, why are you helping me?'

He smiled in wry self-mockery. 'I really don't know,' he mused. 'It must be some kind of temporary insanity.' He stroked the pad of his thumb lightly across the trembling fullness of her mouth. 'Sheer wickedness,' he murmured smokily, his head bending over hers. 'If ever the devil created a woman to tempt mankind...'

'Are you coming or not, Amory?' demanded Sir George impatiently, pushing open the door.

Reluctantly he let her go. 'I'll be right with you, George,' he conceded. 'Mind you stay inside,' he added seriously to Rae. 'Don't leave until I get back, whatever happens.' And then he was gone, with Sir George, leaving her standing forlornly at the window, watching as they stepped into the consul's powerful car and drove away.

# CHAPTER THREE

LADY HAVERING rustled back into the room, bearing a small—a very small—glass of sherry and a few niblets on a silver tray. 'So how long have you known Lord Amory?' she enquired, condescending to play the gracious hostess.

Rae stared at her in shock, the tiny sherry glass almost slipping from her fingers. *Lord* Amory...? 'I—er—we just met tonight,' she managed to stammer.

'Oh?' Those finely drawn eyebrows were raised just a fraction of an inch. 'You surprise me.'

Rae recovered to return her a level look, giving as good as she got. 'Do I?' she queried drily.

The thin lips curled into an acid smile. 'Well, perhaps not,' she conceded with worldly understanding. 'Though I must say I hadn't expected it of Daniel. I know he has something of a raffish reputation, of course, but I never imagined he was the sort to...' She let the sentence drift away, though her meaning was abundantly plain. 'Well, do make yourself comfortable,' she added, forcing herself to extend the polite invitation. 'I'm sure they won't be long.'

She withdrew majestically from the room, closing the door behind her, leaving Rae gasping in fury. 'Old cow,' she muttered with satisfying venom, pulling a face at the gleaming panelled mahogany.

She couldn't drink the sherry—she hated it sweet. To pass the time she drifted along the tanks of tropical fish, admiring their jewel-bright colours. But her eyes strayed again and again to the heavy ormolu carriage clock on the mantelpiece. It was well past midnight. What was happening? Would Daniel manage to get the others out of the gorilla's clutches? She felt sure that he would—somehow he seemed the sort of man who could do anything.

But she couldn't help worrying. She sat down in the chair where she had sat earlier, kicking off her shoes and tucking her feet up beneath her, her strong white teeth chewing at her full lower lip— that nervous habit that Daniel had commented on.

So—her gallant rescuer had turned out to be a lord, no less! Well, she had known he was out of her league from the start—it was a waste of time even dreaming about him. And he had made it abundantly plain what he wanted from her. Sex.

Men! They were all the same, duke or dustman— they were only after one thing. She, more than most, should know that. Oh, there was supposed to be no shame in being illegitimate any more, but the knowledge that you were the product of some man's fleeting satisfaction, and that he hadn't even been bothered to care about your existence, was not very pleasant.

Her mother had been just twenty when she was born—the same age as Rae was now. It hadn't been easy for her, struggling to make a life for herself and her illegitimate daughter. She had taught dancing, eventually establishing her own school, and last year she had finally got married.

It wasn't until Rae had reached adolescence that she had given much thought to the circumstances of her birth. The most humiliating thing was that everyone else knew too—the senior boys in school who used to flock after her, thinking she would be an easy touch; the teacher who had caught her being kissed by the head boy behind the library, and had looked at her with such scorn, as if she were the cheapest kind of slut.

She had vowed right then that she would never repeat the mistake her mother had made—she wouldn't trust any man until she had a ring on her finger. But what she had never taken into account was that she might meet a man who could fill her with a longing so intense that it was beyond all her power to control.

But control it she would, she asserted to herself. Soon the others would be back, and they could make arrangements to fly home straight away. And once they were back in England . . . she would never see him again. A small twist of pain caught at her heart, but her mouth was set in a grim line of resolution. She meant it. She wasn't going to be any man's plaything.

They *would* be back soon, wouldn't they...? She glanced again at the clock. Could anything have gone wrong? She was quite sure the gorilla and his men carried guns. Surely with the police there, and the British consul, they wouldn't start a fight? But this wasn't England—they didn't seem to play by the rules she was used to...

The sound of a car turning into the drive brought her swiftly to her feet, and she ran over to the window. Thank goodness—it was the consul's Daimler. And behind it were two police cars. As the door of the Daimler opened, and Mel scrambled out, she hurried out to the front door and down the steps.

'Mel! Oh, thank goodness, you're safe,' she cried, hugging her friend. 'Are the others all here?'

'Yes. But what happened? One minute——'

'I told you to stay inside!' Roughly Daniel grabbed Rae's arm and hustled her without ceremony back into the house.

She stared up at him in shock. 'What? There's no need to shout at me like that,' she protested, rubbing the bruises on her arm. 'I was only——'

'You're safe in here,' he interrupted her impatiently. 'You've got diplomatic protection.'

'Diplomatic protection? But...?' She looked at him as if he had gone slightly mad. But then over his shoulder she saw the police, six of them, all armed, held at bay on the bottom step by Sir George at his most bombastic. 'What's going on?' she asked, suddenly sensing trouble.

The other girls had piled into the hall, and they gathered around, all talking at once. 'Oh, Rae, it was awful—he shouted and bawled, and he wasn't going to let us go. He said you've stolen some money.'

'He *what*?'

'Your gorilla is claiming you've made off with the contents of his safe,' Daniel explained succinctly.

For a moment she thought her knees were going to give way. 'But that's ridiculous!' she protested, aghast. 'You know I didn't steal anything. Tell them.'

His dark eyes searched hers for one long moment, just as they had earlier when he had asked himself if she were just a good actress. But whatever he saw seemed to satisfy him. 'You've caused him a great deal of trouble,' he pointed out grimly. 'It looks as though he's out to get his own back. This could get very dirty.'

She felt a rising tide of panic inside her. 'You won't let them arrest me—you won't let them put me in prison?' she pleaded, gripping his arm.

He smiled down at her with wry sympathy. 'Don't worry, they won't put you in prison—not if I can help it,' he assured her. 'Come on, let's go into George's office and see if we can get this sorted out.'

Numbly she let him lead her back into the oak-panelled room. Sir George had permitted the two most senior of the police officers to accompany them inside, on condition that they didn't bring their guns. Rae shrank back in her chair, comforted by the powerful presence of Daniel standing behind her, one hand resting lightly on her shoulder as if signalling that she was under his protection. The other girls—and Lady Havering, who was hovering with well-bred curiosity in the background—drifted in behind them, anxiously watching what was going on.

Rae couldn't understand a word of what was being said. A three-way argument, conducted in the unfamiliar language of the islands—haltingly on Sir George's part, fluently and with growing annoyance on Daniel's—seemed to be taking place. She looked from one to the other, bewildered.

'It's really beyond my power to intervene,' protested Sir George, breaking into English to protest to Daniel. 'This is a serious criminal matter—I can't let her stay here. That would be overstepping my authority.'

'So you're just going to let them bang her up in that hell-hole down there?' Daniel demanded, a scathing edge to his voice. 'Anything could happen to her!'

Sir George shook his head, his jaw set in an obstinate line. 'We have to allow the due process of law——'

'Due process be damned!' exploded Daniel, close to losing his temper. 'You know she'll never get a fair trial out here.'

Sir George cast an anxious glance at the policeman to see if he understood this slight on the integrity of the justice system of the islands. 'Look, what if I can get them to release her on bail as soon as she's been charged?' he suggested, increasingly desperate to wheedle his way out from between the rock and the hard place in which he was caught.

Rae bit her lip, watching them all for some clue to what they were saying as they lapsed back into the local language again.

Some solution seemed at last to have been reached, though Daniel plainly wasn't pleased. 'All right,' he conceded tightly. 'But I'm coming with her—and I'm not letting her out of my sight.'

White-faced, she lifted her eyes to his. 'What's happening?' she whispered.

'We're going down to the police station. They're going to formally charge you...' she gasped in horror '...but they'll let you go. I'll stand bail for you.'

She didn't know what to say. It was obviously the best compromise he could win, and at least she wouldn't be left alone in the police station tonight—so long as they kept their word. But what was going to happen? Criminal charges, a court case—what if they found her guilty, and sent her to prison? Here, thousands of miles from home, with no one to watch out for her.

'Thank you,' she murmured belatedly, realising that he had done his best, and was standing by her.

He slid a protective arm around her slim shoulders. 'Come on,' he encouraged. 'We'll go in your car, George.'

Sir George nodded wearily, and rose to his feet. 'I suppose so,' he conceded reluctantly. 'I've given up any hope of getting to bed tonight.'

It would have been a nightmare at the police station without Daniel there beside her. It was an awful building, in the dingiest part of town, as shabby and dilapidated as any of the other buildings, littered with the flotsam and jetsam of the underside of the night.

They were taken into a large office, crowded with about twenty desks and numerous filing cabinets and piles of paper. Every available surface was cluttered with overflowing ashtrays and empty paper cups; smirking policemen were lounging around, and she could feel their eyes crawling all over her until Daniel lent her his jacket to put on over the skimpy dress.

They had to wait quite a time while the policeman made his report. Rae hugged the jacket around her, feeling somehow safer within its enveloping folds. A subtle musky aroma clung to the fabric, reminding her with every breath of the way it had felt to be held in Daniel's strong arms.

At last a bored-looking plain-clothes detective came over, sitting down at one of the desks and pulling a battered-looking typewriter towards him. 'OK, let's get this down,' he drawled in an accent culled from too many cheap American movies. 'You just got here last night, right?'

Rae answered his questions, relieved that at least he spoke English, though he needed frequent translations from Daniel over difficult words. Sir George had found himself a chair and sat down, after fastidiously dusting it off with his handkerchief, and was regarding the proceedings with an air of refined distaste.

They insisted on taking her fingerprints and her photograph, making her stand against a blank wall holding a board with a number on it in front of her. She turned desperate eyes to Daniel, but he couldn't help her—he could only smile reassuringly, standing with his arms folded across his chest, his whole presence a warning that at least appeared to restrain them from treating her too roughly.

At last it seemed to be over. Daniel had read through her statement, and agreed that she should sign it, and then there was another wait while the detective took the papers to his superior. Rae stood chewing her lip, too agitated to sit down, until he returned.

'What if they won't let me go?' she asked, her voice unsteady.

'Don't worry.' Daniel drew her into his arms. 'It'll be all right.'

She leaned her forehead gratefully against his wide shoulder, and his hand stroked over her hair, stilling the trembling that was racking her body. She had never felt more frightened in her life—if he hadn't been there, she was sure she would have just gone to pieces.

At last the detective came back, and ushered them upstairs into a large, imposing office—the funds for the entire precinct seemed to have been channelled into providing the opulent decorations and furniture. Behind a vast desk of gleaming mahogany, toying with a carved ivory paper knife, was a thickset man in a uniform covered with the gold braid of senior rank. He was studying the papers the detective had handed him, an expression of grave disapproval on his face, and he didn't invite them to sit down.

'Well,' he said at last, fixing Rae with a pinning stare from one basilisk eye—the other, she realised, was glass.

Cold fingers of fear gripped at her heart, and unconsciously she reached for Daniel's hand. The touch of his strong fingers gave her the courage to keep her head up. The police chief's eye flickered to Daniel, and he glanced at the papers again.

'So—you're offering to stand surety for this— er—young lady,' he said, allowing the faintest hint of surprise to infiltrate his voice.

'Yes.'

'Hmm.' That single eye drifted over her again in unmistakable contempt. 'However, I'm not at all sure that I'm prepared to grant bail. In my experience, women of this sort are not to be trusted. The best place for her is one of my cells.'

Daniel's arm came protectively around her shoulders. 'Your officers promised that she wouldn't be detained,' he insisted, his voice hard. 'It was only on that understanding that we agreed to come here.'

The police chief shook his head, his tone spuriously sympathetic. 'Take my advice, my friend,' he suggested. 'Find yourself another little pussy-cat to play with. In Kahyangan there are many to choose from.' He spread his hands in an expansive gesture. 'Leave this one to us.'

The way he looked at her brought a sudden choke of nausea to Rae's throat—she could have little doubt what would happen to her if Daniel left her here. But his strong arm was supporting her, and that air of natural authority gave notice that he would not be opposed.

'For your information,' he announced levelly, 'Miss Dillon is my fiancée.'

Rae blinked in shock, but before she could make a sound Daniel squeezed her shoulders in warning. She bit back the protest she had been about to utter, and drew herself up with dignity, trying hard to look as if the character fitted her, in spite of the cheap tackiness of her clothes.

The police chef eyed them both suspiciously—he plainly wasn't entirely convinced, but he was too wary to take the chance that it might be true. Whoever Daniel was, Rae reflected with a touch of asperity, he was certainly important enough to carry a fair amount of clout even in this unholy place.

'I see.' The police chief shot a furious glance at the detective from his one disconcerting eye, clearly blaming him for placing him in this awkward position. 'Well, in that case, of course...' Reluctantly he took a thick gold pen from his desk, and scrawled a signature across the bottom of one of the papers. 'Bail is set at fifty thousand rupals.'

Rae gasped—it was a ridiculous amount, more than five times what she was accused of having stolen. But Daniel didn't bat an eyelid. 'Very well,' he agreed. 'Where do I sign?'

In a kind of daze Rae watched as he signed the papers, and within a few moments she found herself once more ensconced on the luxurious Connolly hide upholstery of the honorary consul's Daimler.

'My goodness!' she breathed in heartfelt relief. 'I was beginning to think I'd never get out of there!'

'Unfortunately that's only the first hurdle,' Daniel remarked drily. 'You can't stay on the island—not unless you want that gorilla of yours to come looking for you.'

'Oh, lord!' She bit her lip. 'I hadn't even thought of that. But what can I do? I haven't even got my passport—and besides, I can't jump bail. You'd lose all that money.'

He slanted her a cynical glance. 'Does that bother you? It's my money, and I can well afford it.'

'That's not the point.' She flashed him a look of angry indignation. He still thought the worst of her—would nothing convince him that he was wrong?

'And George would issue you with an emergency passport,' he added, as if trying to lure her into betraying herself. 'Wouldn't you, George?'

'No, I most certainly would not!' exploded that gentleman from the front seat. 'A representative of Her Majesty's Government, abetting a fugitive to escape from justice? I'm afraid it's quite impossible!'

Daniel shrugged, as if he had been expecting that answer. 'Well, then, we'll just have to think of a way to persuade them to drop the charges,' he mused, his dark eyes thoughtful as he considered the problem.

'I don't think they're very likely to do that,' put in Rae. 'He was a nasty piece of work, that policeman. You could tell what he thought of me—and he certainly didn't believe we were really engaged.'

Sir George gave a snort of sardonic amusement.

'Well, George,' enquired Daniel, a sharp edge in his voice, 'Have you got any useful suggestions?'

'Me? It's nothing more to do with me, I've fulfilled my duty,' he insisted. 'I can wash my hands of the whole affair now. You're the one who's set on playing the hero.' He chuckled with malicious laughter. 'If you're so concerned about her welfare, maybe you'd better take the thing to its logical conclusion, and marry her,' he taunted. 'They couldn't deny a marriage certificate, and I don't think they're very likely to want to prosecute so important a person as the wife of Lord Amory for petty theft. They'd probably drop all the charges, and apologise for causing her so much inconvenience.'

The acid sarcasm in his voice made Rae's cheeks flush with scarlet, but to her surprise Daniel began to laugh. 'You know, you could have a point there, George,' he agreed, his voice lazily mocking—though whether it was directed at the honorary consul or at himself, Rae couldn't tell. 'Maybe I'll do just that.'

She stared at him in horror. 'But . . . we can't!' she protested, dumbfounded.

'Why not?' he countered, as coolly as if the suggestion were utterly reasonable. 'Are you already married?'

'No, but——'

'Nor am I, so there's nothing to stop us.'

Her mind was spinning in a whirlpool of confusion. 'But we can't just go off and get married,' she objected, struggling to keep some grip on her sanity. 'I mean... well...'

He lifted one dark eyebrow in sardonic enquiry. 'Can you think of a better idea?'

'Well, no—not just at the moment,' she admitted. 'But... there must be *some* other way, surely?'

'If you can think of one, we'll try it,' he offered cordially. 'But it had better be soon—the longer you're here on the island the greater the chance that your gorilla will come after you and try to snatch you back.'

She sat back in her corner of the car, her numb brain struggling to make sense of the crazy mess she had landed herself in. The thought of what might happen to her at the hands of the man who owned the Paradise club was too horrific to contemplate—almost any alternative was preferable to that.

But to marry Daniel? It was outrageous—she had known him for only a few hours... And she shouldn't let him do it—what on earth would his family think? They would be appalled. Of course they would be able to get it annulled as soon as they got back to England, but even so... And if the newspapers got hold of it they would have a field-day with it.

But what else could she do? She *couldn't* let him forfeit all that money—fifty thousand rupals was more than she could ever pay him back if she worked forty-eight hours a day for the rest of her life. And she couldn't trust the police—they would more than likely just hand her over to the gorilla as soon as Daniel was gone. They could just say she had escaped or something...

She was no nearer to reaching a solution to her problem when the car turned in through some tall iron gates, guarded by smartly liveried security personnel, and drew to a halt before the wide glass entrance to a very swish hotel. A uniformed commissionaire in white kid gloves stepped forward and opened the door.

Daniel followed her from the car, turning to close the door behind him. 'Goodnight, George,' he drawled, a sardonic inflexion in his voice. 'Thank you for your unstinting support.'

'Hrmph!'

As the Daimler swept away, Rae gazed up at the building, her mouth twisting into a wry smile. She should have known that Daniel would be staying at the most expensive hotel in town; a newly built edifice of glass and concrete, overlooking the harbour and the bay. She held back, reluctant to follow him up the steps.

'What's wrong?' he asked.

'Me,' she pointed out, flickering an unhappy glance at her own reflection in the glass doors. The dress was so short that the hem barely showed beneath Daniel's jacket, and the low-cut neckline was hidden behind the revers. 'I look as if I haven't got anything on under this.'

A sudden heat flamed in his eyes, and she felt the colour in her cheeks deepen. She hadn't intended to be provocative—the words had come out quite unthinkingly. 'Perhaps we'd better find you something a little more respectable to wear,' he conceded, though his tone suggested that he preferred the show of her long slender legs.

He took her arm, and steered her into the hotel. There was a night manager on duty in reception, and he greeted them with polite deference—if he had any opinion about one of his guests returning in the middle of the night in the company of a young lady whose state of clothing suggested that she might not be of the strictest virtue, he kept his thoughts discreetly to himself.

Rae gazed around the imposing foyer in awe. She had never seen anything so magnificent: an acre of white marble, filled with an exotic jungle of greenery, complete with an indoor waterfall that tumbled down from a veranda two floors above, and a mall of smart boutiques stocking the most expensive jewellery and perfumes and designer clothes from around the world.

'Are you hungry?' Daniel asked her.

'Starving!' With some surprise, she realised that the last proper meal she had eaten had been on the plane, thirty-six hours ago.

'Come on, then—I'd better feed you,' said Daniel with a smile, taking her arm. 'By the time we've eaten, someone will be here to open one of the shops for you.'

She stared at him, aghast. 'You've made them drag someone out in the middle of the night just to open up for me?' she protested.

'The shop's owned by a cousin of the night manager,' he explained patiently. 'They would never pass up the opportunity of making a sale, whatever the time of night.'

'Besides, I couldn't possibly afford anything from the shops in here,' she argued.

'You don't have to—call it a wedding present.'

'No.' She shook her head firmly. 'I owe you quite enough already that I can never repay. I can't let you spend money on me as well.'

A spark of sardonic humour flickered in the depths of his dark eyes. 'All right, I'll lend you the money,' he conceded. 'You can pay me back whenever you can afford it.'

She hesitated, uncertain. She had to have clothes—she couldn't go on walking around looking like this. If she stuck to the absolute minimum . . . Once she got back to England she could get a job— anything would do—and she was used to living cheaply.

'Very well.' She nodded reluctantly. 'But you must promise to make a note of everything you spend—for food and for that taxi as well. I don't know how long it'll take me to pay you.'

'Don't worry,' he assured her with a dry smile. 'I won't charge you too much interest.'

The coffee-lounge was beside the jungle of indoor greenery, with comfortable wicker chairs, and rich aromatic coffee served by a reed-slim oriental girl in an elegant white silk cheong-sam. The chef came out from his kitchen to find out what Rae would like to eat—she settled for tender shredded chicken cooked in coconut milk, served with delicately spiced rice and a deliciously savoury peanut sauce.

She had just finished the meal when another slender girl approached them, bowing charmingly. 'When *madame* is ready, my shop is open,' she invited in a soft voice.

'Oh...thank you.' She glanced fleetingly at Daniel; such was the service his money could buy. No wonder he was so accustomed to getting his own way. Was he going to be angry when he found out that even after all he had done for her she was going to refuse to go to bed with him?

The clothes in the small shop were beautiful—jewel-coloured silks, soft knitted cashmeres, the finest embroidered lawn. But none of them had a price on—it was one of those places where if you had to ask how much a thing cost, you couldn't afford it. Gingerly she began to look along the rails, searching for something that might not bankrupt her for more than six months.

'Is *madame* looking for something special?' enquired the proprietress with a deference that still retained its own serene dignity.

'Something not too expensive,' Rae confessed, slightly desperate. 'Do you have any jeans?'

'I have some cotton trousers,' the girl suggested, reaching for a hanger.

'Oh, yes—those will do very well,' agreed Rae with relief. 'Now I just need a T-shirt or something.'

'How about this?' suggested Daniel. He had chosen a top of fine knitted cotton, embroidered with a satin appliqué flower. The colour was a soft raspberry pink that Rae knew at once would be perfect—but not many men would have picked that shade so unerringly, especially with her red hair. He must have had a good deal of experience in helping to choose women's clothes, she reflected wryly.

'And you'll want some underwear,' he added, a glint of wickedness in his eyes.

She felt her cheeks flame scarlet. 'Oh, no—I can manage...'

But he ignored her protests, strolling down to the far end of the shop where the daintiest confections of silk and lace were temptingly displayed. 'Are these your size?' he asked, making a carefully considered selection from among the items on show.

'Er—yes.' She took them from him quickly, and retreated to the changing-room, crimson with embarrassment.

It was a relief to get out of that tacky dress. She dropped it on to the floor, and kicked it viciously into a corner. Then she hesitated, looking at the expensive set of lingerie that Daniel had chosen for her. A small shimmer of heat ran through her. He must have studied her body in some detail to have guessed her size so accurately...

But she *did* need to change—and they were so beautiful: a camisole bra, and French knickers of sheerest ivory silk, trimmed with the most delicate ivory-tinted lace. Slowly, still half at war in her mind, she stripped off her own cheap things, and tossed them aside with the dress.

For a moment she stood, surrounded by the dazzling reflection of half a dozen brightly lit mirrors that showed her her image from every side. She was used to looking at her body—every day at dance practice she studied every line, knowing herself from every angle and in every position. But somehow she seemed to be seeing herself for the first time.

This was what Daniel wanted to possess—every soft, naked curve; her breasts, their firm swell invitingly tipped with ripe buds of pink, the smooth contours of her stomach, the slender length of her thighs, crowned with that small cluster of curls the colour of rosewood, hiding the sensual secrets within...

And deep inside her, some primeval core of feminine submissiveness ached to surrender to her fate, even though she knew that for him it would be no more than a fleeting affair, a casual fling with some dancer he had met in some far-off place, far removed from the world he usually moved in.

At least, that was what it *would* have been. But now it was even worse—the complications of marrying him didn't bear thinking about! If she could simply have been his mistress... Just for a moment, she let her mind indulge the tempting fantasy, drawing on the soft silk lingerie, imagining that he was standing there watching her.

Oh, it was so lovely—she had never worn silk against her skin before, and the touch of it was like a caress. And there was something so... intimate about wearing underwear he had bought, even though she intended to pay him back every penny. All the time she was wearing it, she would be conscious that he, in a sense, owned it—as if that conferred on him some sort of rights over the body inside...

Her mouth felt suddenly dry, and she shook her head briskly to clear it of the dangerous dream. Quickly she got dressed in the cream cotton trousers and the pink top, and checked her reflection one last time in the mirrors. At least she looked a little more presentable now.

Daniel was leaning negligently against the counter, waiting for her, but as he saw her he straightened, his eyes registering unmistakable approval. 'Very nice,' he murmured with a slow, possessive smile. 'Turn around.'

She obeyed, conscious of his assessing gaze on every inch of her body. She knew what he was thinking—that she was his for the taking. She could hardly blame him for that—she was all too uncomfortably aware that she had given him every reason to believe that she would be more than ready to comply.

What would he do when she refused? Would he leave her to take her chances between the gorilla and the police? Surely he wouldn't be that ruthless...? And yet... A nervous glance at that hard profile sent a shimmer of chill down her spine. He was a man who expected to get what he had paid for, down to the last penny. And though he hadn't actually paid for her in cash...

Somehow she managed an unsteady laugh. 'I feel a lot better than I did in that awful dress, anyway,' she remarked. She turned to the young shop-owner, hovering with polite self-effacement in the background. 'Could you tell me how much these things cost, please?' she enquired, bracing herself to hear the worst.

The poor girl looked quite shocked that she should ask, lifting her eyes to Daniel in an anxious question. He nodded assent. 'Altogether, one hundred and eighty-five rupals.'

Rae drew in a deep breath, making a rapid calculation in her head. She needed to be no genius of mathematics to realise just how long it was going to take her to pay Daniel back—always supposing that she could find a job when she got back to England.

'Thank you,' she said with a sinking heart. Every step seemed to be taking her deeper into the labyrinth, and it was becoming harder and harder to see any way out of it.

# CHAPTER FOUR

THEY didn't speak as the lift rode up smoothly to the top floor. The doors slid open, and they stepped out into a wide octagonal hall, the floor tiled in rich terracotta, the walls panelled in gleaming wood. There were just two pairs of double doors, one on each side, and Rae waited, her heart pounding, as Daniel inserted his card-key into one of the locks.

The suite was on the grand scale—it almost took her breath away: a wide expanse of the same terracotta floor-tiles, deep comfortable sofas upholstered in soft tan hide, and one long wall of glass that gave a panoramic view over the whole town. She walked across to gaze out at the scene.

Below them swept the deep curve of the harbour; sampan restaurants floated at anchor in the typhoon shelter, their coloured paper lanterns reflecting brightly in the water. Lights blazed in the smart hotels and office blocks that climbed the slopes to the west, and beyond rose the towering shadow of Tikuan Peak, dark and mysterious against the night sky.

'Pretty spectacular, isn't it?'

He had come up very close behind her, and she felt again that strange tension that seemed to shimmer in the air between them, like the warning heat before a thunderstorm. She lifted her eyes to look at his face, and knew that he was aware of it too.

'Yes, I . . .' She side-stepped evasively, conscious of the faint tinge of pink in her cheeks. 'What time is it?'

'A little after three.'

'Oh . . .' A kind of desperation was rising inside her. She was alone with him, in this luxurious suite, in the middle of the night. How on earth could she ever keep things under control? 'Are Mel and the others staying in this hotel too?' she enquired, her voice over-bright.

He laughed drily. 'I very much doubt it. George will have fixed them up with something—they'll be here in the morning.'

'Oh . . . good.'

He reached for her hand. 'In the meantime . . .' he murmured softly, drawing her across the room and pushing open a door.

With a thud of panic her eyes took in a huge bed, fully six feet wide, covered in a quilted satin spread. 'I . . . I'm sorry. I don't . . . I mean, I wouldn't want you to think . . .' She bit her lip, gazing up at him. 'I can't . . .'

One dark eyebrow lifted by a fraction of an inch. 'I don't expect you to,' he responded, an inflexion of sardonic humour in his voice. 'But it's been a long night, and I don't know about you, but I could do with a little sleep.'

'Sleep?'

'Yes, sleep.' He drew her into his arms, holding her loosely so that she could easily have escaped if she had wanted to. 'For tonight. After all, there's no rush, is there?'

His warm lips brushed over her temple, and then before she could protest any further he had scooped her up and carried her over to the bed, nestling her into the crook of his arm as he lay down beside her. 'There,' he murmured coaxingly. 'Isn't that better?'

Rae was quivering with tension, her heartbeat racing out of control. His body was lean and hard against hers, and his hand was stroking over her hair, as if he were soothing a nervous kitten. She closed her eyes, letting the faint evocative muskiness of his skin inveigle her senses.

She couldn't fight it; the longing inside her was too powerful for her to handle. She belonged to him, more surely than if he had paid that fifty rupals for one night with her. Love had bought her for ever—even though she knew he wouldn't want her for that long.

But slowly she began to realise that his breathing had become deep and slow, and his hand had stilled. She opened her eyes cautiously, and looked at him. Dark silky lashes, startlingly in contrast to the hard lines of his face, shadowed his cheeks. He was asleep.

She gazed at him, bound by a strange spell. She was frightened of him, but not in the same way as she was frightened of the gorilla. What he had been doing in that night-club, and why he had apparently been prepared to pay money to spend the night with her, she didn't know, but she was as sure as

she was of her own name that he had had no more
intention of following through that little charade
than she had.

No, what scared her about him was the way he
made her feel. She was falling in love with him.
And tomorrow—or rather later today—unless one
of them could think of some other solution she
would be marrying him. But it wouldn't be real.
As soon as they got back to England, it would have
to be annulled. One single tear trickled from the
corner of her eye, and traced a path down her
cheek.

Daniel lay very still, willing his breathing to remain
steady in spite of the effect it was having on him
to hold that warm soft body in his arms. He really
hadn't had any intention of making love to her tonight—anyone could see that she was worn out. But
her reaction when he had brought her in here had
surprised him. Why had she put on that virginal
act? No girl who kissed the way she did could be
lacking in experience.

And yet he was pretty sure she wasn't the kind
of girl she had first appeared...or was he letting
his hunger for that tempting mouth of hers lure
him into making a massive misjudgement of her
character? He knew that if he were wrong about
her it could cost him a pretty big headache.

But he didn't want to think about that tonight.
He'd decided to take the gamble, and if it led to
trouble he'd let his lawyers worry about sorting it
out—that was what they were paid for. All he

wanted to do for now was hold her, and smell again the sweet fragrance of her hair. They would make love soon—he had absolutely no doubt of that. And it was going to be good.

Rae woke to the rattle of coffee-cups, and sat up in alarm as a white-liveried waiter wheeled a room-service trolley into the bedroom. Daniel was behind him—he had changed into a clean white shirt and pale grey trousers, and his dark hair curled damply from his shower.

'Good morning, sleepyhead,' he greeted her. 'I thought you might like some breakfast.'

'Oh!' Her cheeks flamed scarlet—what assumptions must the waiter be making? 'Thank you,' she stammered, slipping off the bed and moving quickly over to a wicker armchair by the window, as if disowning all responsibility for her share of the rumpled satin quilt and dented pillows.

Daniel slipped the waiter a discreet tip, and came over to join her, folding his long frame into the other chair and surveying the trolley with interest. 'Try some of the fruit,' he suggested. 'It's delicious.'

'Th—thank you.' Slices of the moist, delicate fruit—papaya, melon, pineapple, kiwi—had been arranged with great care to form flower patterns on the plate. 'It seems almost a pity to spoil it,' she remarked, trying to match the lightness of his manner.

How did you make polite conversation with a man over the breakfast table? It wasn't a situation she had ever been in before. Feeling awkward and naïve, she couldn't think of a thing to say, and turned her attention instead to gaze out of the window.

The sun had burned away the early-morning mist, and the view was breathtaking. The sea was a pure azure blue, reflecting the blue of the sky. Across the bay, the tree-clad slopes of Tikuan Peak rose above the glittering white towers of the town.

'What a beautiful place!' she breathed.

'Yes, it is. It's a pity you've seen only the underside of it—you should have had a chance to see more of the island.'

She smiled grimly. 'I don't think I will,' she said. 'The sooner I get away from here, the happier I'll be.'

He nodded in agreement. 'I know someone who I think will be able to help us there,' he told her. She looked up at him, hope springing in her eyes. 'He's a priest—he runs a mission hospital over on the southern peninsula, but he can perform marriages as well.'

'Oh...' She lowered her eyes to her plate. 'I was hoping...maybe you might have thought of something else by now.'

'I'm sorry to disappoint you—I'm afraid it seems to be the only way.'

'Oh, well.' She shrugged her slim shoulders, struggling to give the impression that it mattered as little to her as it apparently did to him. 'I suppose we'll have to go through with it, then.'

'You don't have to sound so reluctant,' he re-marked with a dry laugh. 'It doesn't have to be forever.'

'Oh, no, of course not,' she agreed at once. 'It'll be quite easy to get it annulled as soon as we get back to England, won't it?'

'No problem.'

She nodded dumbly, sipping her coffee, trying hard to hide the foolish sense of disappointment she was feeling. They were getting *married* for goodness' sake—didn't it mean *anything* to him? Oh, she was just being a romantic idiot—it was nothing more than an expedient, a way to get her out of the country. But she couldn't help dreaming...

Draining her coffee-cup, she rose to her feet. 'Well, I think I'll go and have a shower,' she said, hoping he wouldn't notice the tremor in her voice. 'I expect the others will be here soon.'

She made her escape quickly to the bathroom, locking the door behind her and leaning against it, closing her eyes on the unwelcome tears that were welling up. She really ought to be grateful to him for going to such extraordinary lengths to help her, not resenting the fact that he could treat it all with such casual unconcern.

If only there were some other way out... But what? The police certainly wouldn't drop the charges for a mere Miss Dillon, a cabaret dancer, a nobody. But for Mrs Daniel Amory—no, *Lady* Daniel Amory, she corrected herself wryly—nothing would be impossible.

She opened her eyes, and gazed around the bathroom. Even in here there were those little touches of luxury that told her she had stepped into another world—the gold-plated taps, the marble bath, the fragrant arrangement of tropical grasses and flowers on the vanity unit.

But she didn't belong; she could never belong in Daniel's life. Oh, yes, he wanted her—but not as his wife. He would have been more than happy to make her his mistress—he had made that plain enough. But she couldn't be that, either. Once they got back to England, and had made arrangements to annul this sham marriage, she would have to say goodbye to him, and never see him again.

And that, she knew, was going to be the hardest thing she had ever done. But the alternative would be even more painful. Every moment she stayed with him, every night she shared his bed, would etch her love deeper into her heart, until the inevitable parting would tear her apart.

She spent as long as she possibly could in the bathroom to avoid the awkwardness of being alone with him. It wasn't until she heard noises that indicated that the other girls had arrived that she finally unlocked the door and emerged.

'Rae!' Mel squeaked with delight when she saw her, and threw her arms around her, hugging her. 'Oh, my goodness. I was afraid they'd arrested you!' Her sparkling sapphire-blue eyes swept around the room in awe. 'What a place this is,' she whispered, none too quietly. 'I've never seen anything like it—he must be *loaded*! And where did you get those clothes? Did *he* buy them for you?'

'No,' insisted Rae, colouring slightly. 'He's just lent me the money—I'll pay him back as soon as I can.'

Mel looked at her as if she were slightly mad. 'Pay him back? What on earth for? I mean, it's not as though it's a fur coat or something.'

'That's beside the point.'

'I wish I had a man to buy me smashing things like that,' sighed Mel enviously. 'You're dead lucky.'

Rae smiled wryly to herself—it wouldn't be easy to explain her scruples to her friend. It wasn't that Mel was amoral—just that she tended to sail sublimely through life, rarely troubled by second thoughts.

The suite impressed the other girls every bit as much as it had Mel, but they soon made themselves at home, draping themselves around on the comfortable furniture with studied elegance. Daniel called up room service for more coffee, and if the waiter thought it a little odd to find *five* leggy young ladies in occupation he didn't betray his curiosity by so much as a flicker.

'Mmm—I could get used to this,' sighed Liz, slanting Daniel a bright-eyed look from beneath her lashes. 'It must cost an absolute *fortune* to stay here.'

'It isn't cheap,' he confirmed drily. 'Fortunately it rates as a legitimate business expense.'

'You mean your firm pays?' queried Liz, a shade disappointed.

'I'm afraid so.'

'What do you do?' Angie put in—even if he wasn't paying for the suite himself, he was the best-looking man she had ever laid eyes on. OK, so Rae had seen him first, but there was absolutely nothing wrong with being friendly, was there?

'I'm an investment banker,' he responded, a flicker of amusement lurking in the depths of his eyes.

'A banker?' Cathy leaned back in the corner of her seat, crossing her elegant legs so that he could appreciate their shapeliness all the better. 'I always thought that was terribly dull.' Why don't you convince me otherwise? her eyes invited.

Rae sat quietly, trying not to feel a twinge of jealousy as her friends competed with each other to flirt with him, each in their individual way—Mel all breathless admiration, Liz vivacious, Angie exotic, Cathy cool and come-hither.

He was obviously responding—who could blame him? They were all very attractive girls. What if he should decide that he preferred one of them to her? Perhaps that would be the best thing, she tried to convince herself. And, after all, she could hardly complain about losing him when she had never really had him in the first place.

'Anyway, tell us all about what happened last night,' Mel was insisting eagerly. 'How on earth did you manage to get out?'

'Ah—that's quite a story.' Daniel related the events briefly, his eyes mocking at Rae as he told how she had knocked him out with the champagne bottle.

'Oh, Rae, you didn't!' gasped Mel. 'Oh, what an awful thing to do.' She turned all the dazzle of her huge sapphire-blue eyes on Daniel—that look had been known to melt the strongest men. 'She didn't hurt you, did she?'

'Not a great deal,' he assured her, not immune to that sweetly feminine concern.

'When the two of you went off like that—well, we didn't know what to think,' Mel fluttered.

'Oh, yes, you did,' Liz reminded her scathingly. 'In fact, you'd have gone off yourself with that creep you were with, if we hadn't all agreed to stick together.'

'No, I wouldn't,' protested Mel, hurt. 'And besides, he wasn't a creep, he was very nice.'

'Oh, do stop bickering, you two,' drawled Cathy with lofty disdain. 'So what are you going to do now, Rae? Surely you won't have to stay here until they sort all this stupid business out?'

Rae bit her lip. Somehow she couldn't quite bring herself to say the words. But Daniel spoke for her. 'She can't stay here—it would be far too dangerous for her on her own. So we're employing a little subtle strategy.' His lip curled into a sardonic smile as Rae squirmed uncomfortably. 'We're getting married. Strictly temporary, of course,' he added as they all gasped in amazement. 'But you're all invited to the wedding.'

'*What*? Getting married? But when?' cried Mel. 'Oh, Rae, you never told me! Well, of all the... Oh, congratulations! I think that's wonderful.'

'It's only to get the police to drop the charges, so I can go home,' Rae reminded her repressively. 'We'll be getting it annulled right away.'

Mel looked confused, and not entirely convinced. 'Oh... I see... But it's still quite romantic, isn't it? I mean, meeting like that, and then... But what on earth are you going to wear?' she added, anxious about the priorities. 'Will you have time to get a proper wedding dress?'

'No, of course not—I won't need one. I told you, it's not a real wedding—just a form.'

The hotel's air-conditioned white limousine held the six of them in comfort; where an English driver might have had a plastic St Christopher dangling from his rear-view mirror for luck, this one had an intricate twist of dried banana leaf and pink lotus flowers, swaying at every turn.

The road wound across the shoulder of the still-active volcano that formed the backbone of the island. On the lower slopes, every available inch of land had been terraced for paddy fields, layer upon intricate layer of them following every contour of the land, sparkling emerald-green beneath the bright tropical sun.

Here and there they passed through small villages, with thatch-roofed wooden houses each with its own small spirit-temple at the door, decorated with colourful offerings of fruit and flowers. Thin white hens scratched idly in the dusty ground, and lazy brown dogs dozed wherever they could find a little shade.

It took a little over half an hour to reach their destination—a tiny fishing village on the southern tip of the island. The wooden houses clustered right down to the shore in an untidy jumble, and out on the clear blue waters of the bay floated dozens of square fish-traps, made from lashed-together oil cans and covered with netting.

The taxi stopped in what was obviously the main square, opposite an old stone jetty where several fishing-junks were moored. A couple of sampans seemed to provide housing for several families each, and at once a swarm of barefoot children appeared as if from nowhere, scrabbling around the car in noisy excitement.

It soon became evident that it was Daniel's arrival that had delighted them. They gathered around him as he climbed from the front seat, swinging on his arms and vying eagerly for his attention. He laughed, swooping up one small boy on to his shoulders, and responding to them all in their own tongue.

The girls followed him from the car, gazing around in fascination and finding themselves also the subject of a certain amount of curiosity from the children. 'They don't get many tourists out here,' Daniel offered by way of an explanation. 'Come on, the mission station is over there.'

On the far side of the square was a weathered palisade fence enclosing a tangled garden and several wooden buildings. Another group of small children, most of them sporting bandages or dressings of some kind, sat beneath the shade of an ancient banyan tree before a blackboard where a tall, grey-clad nun was instructing them in simple sums. As soon as they saw Daniel, their lesson was forgotten.

The nun looked round, laughing when she saw the cause of the interruption. 'I should have known it would be you!' she declared. 'You always ruin my classes.'

'Sorry, Maria,' Daniel apologised easily. 'Is Jimmy around?'

'Father Ignatius is in the dispensary,' she informed him, pretending to scold. She turned her smiling eyes to the girls, as curious as the children. 'Hello. I'm sorry; we don't get many strangers here. You must be hot after your journey—would you like some lemonade? It's home-made. We have a refrigerator for the drugs, but Father Ignatius lets us use a tiny corner of it for cool drinks for our little patients,' she added conspiratorially.

Rae had eased herself to the back of the group, feeling more and more uncomfortable in this situation. If only she could think of some other way out of her predicament! But her mind had gone numb in the heat—it was sweltering hot now, in the full glare of the mid-morning sun, and there was no pleasant chill of air-conditioning here as there was at the hotel.

Mel, however, was suffering from no inhibitions at all. 'Ooh, lemonade would be lovely,' she sighed. 'I could just drink a whole gallon!'

Only by the slightest flicker of consternation did Sister Maria betray her momentary anxiety for the station's stocks, before she sent one of the older children to fetch supplies, and shooed the others back into their alfresco schoolroom.

'This way,' said Daniel, glancing around for Rae. Reluctantly she followed him across the garden and into one of the wooden buildings. The 'dispensary' was a rough table and a chair in the middle of the bare floor, where a queue of mothers and babies were waiting patiently for their turn. But at least it was a little cooler in here, thanks to an electric fan tied with string to one of the cross-beams supporting the roof.

The white-coated doctor glanced up from his work, a broad smile on his face when he saw who had come in. 'Daniel! I thought you were going back to England today?' he greeted him genially.

'A slight hitch,' Daniel answered, an inflexion of wry humour in his voice. 'I've come to ask a favour, Jim.'

'Ask away!' came the generous response.

'I want to get married.'

The good man nearly fell off his chair. 'Married? But...you never said a word about it the other day. What have you been keeping up your sleeve?'

'Nothing,' Daniel assured him, smiling. 'This is Rae Dillon. Rae—Father Ignatius Xavier, Jim.

Renegade priest, quack, and the best fly-fisherman in the whole South China Sea.'

'Less of the renegade,' the priest protested, rising to his feet and punching Daniel playfully on the shoulder. 'And the quack. The praise of my fly-fishing I'll graciously accept. I'm delighted to meet you, young lady,' he added, offering her his hand.

'Thank you,' she murmured, feeling even more embarrassed.

'So, you've finally decided to settle down, then?' enquired Father Ignatius, his pale-blue eyes twinkling up at Daniel. 'I won't say it's before time.'

Rae lifted pleading eyes to Daniel's face, begging him to tell the truth.

'Well—er—actually, Jim, it's not quite like that,' he admitted.

Ginger eyebrows soared in perplexed enquiry.

'Miss Dillon has had the misfortune to run into a little difficulty with a local businessman, and it's rather important that she leaves the country as soon as possible,' Daniel explained succinctly. 'Unfortunately the police are keen to press charges, which makes it a little difficult. So I'm offering her my—er—protection, in the hope that it will persuade them to overlook the matter.'

The young priest frowned, worried. 'Oh, dear,' he fretted, shaking his head. 'I'm really not at all sure I ought to allow myself to be a party to this, Daniel. I wish you hadn't asked me.'

Rae bit her lip. 'I'm sorry,' she pleaded. 'It's just . . . I don't know what else to do. I haven't done anything wrong, honestly, but I can't get the police to believe that. And there's this man who's after me, and if he finds me...' She shuddered as the thought of what might happen to her rose in her mind, like a recurring nightmare.

'Well, yes,' flustered the priest. 'I can quite see that the situation is very serious, but...well, I'm not sure that getting married——'

'It's the only thing that'll convince them to drop the charges,' Daniel argued. 'Just pretending to be engaged wasn't good enough.'

'We'll get it annulled as soon as we get back to England,' Rae put in anxiously.

'Annulled, eh?' But still he hesitated.

Daniel put his hand into his pocket, and drew out his chequebook. 'What was it you were saying to me about a new heart-monitor?' he enquired, his voice casual.

The priest looked shocked. 'Daniel! You're *not* trying to bribe me?' he protested, aghast.

'Not at all,' responded Daniel with a bland smile. 'Just...offering a small donation to the hospital.'

The priest laughed, shaking his head. 'Damn you, Daniel—what about my conscience?' He glanced across to where two frail-looking children were sitting on a step in the shade, and then back at the chequebook in Daniel's hand. 'Very well,' he conceded wryly. 'Um...we could do with some more supplies of X-ray plates, too.'

Daniel nodded, and, taking out a pen, he swiftly wrote out a cheque. The priest took it and tucked it into his pocket without looking at it. 'You'll have to wait until I've finished here—I won't be more than about half an hour. Maria will give you some lemonade. Sometimes I think she's planning to go into the wholesale business, the amount of room she takes up in my drugs fridge!'

They got back to the others to find that all pretence at schooling had been abandoned for the day. The children were in a state of high excitement, and Sister Maria laughingly apologised for them.

'I hope you don't mind—they want to come and see the wedding,' she explained. 'It isn't something that happens very often here.'

'Oh...no, I don't mind,' agreed Rae weakly. It was all happening to someone else anyway—this couldn't be her, about to marry a man she had met less than twenty-four hours ago. As the children danced around her, chattering in complete disregard of the fact that she couldn't understand a word they were saying, she smiled down at them, feeling as though she were walking in a dream.

'They want to put flowers in your hair,' the nun translated for her. 'It's a tradition here for brides. Please let them—it would make them so happy.'

'Of course.'

And so she sat down on the grass beneath the great bearded old banyan, and let them minister to her with their tiny nimble hands, smiling approval as they showed her the choice perfect blooms they had gathered. She had no idea what they were doing to her—two of the older girls had swept her hair up and held it in place with pins, and were weaving the flower stems into it as the younger ones brought them.

In their bright, eager faces she could forget her own anxieties for a while. It was sad to think that most of them were here because they were sick. Just one little mite hung back, reluctant to bring forward the pretty flower he had picked.

'What's wrong with him?' she asked Sister Maria.

'He has leprosy. Of course, it isn't in the infectious stage, or we wouldn't let him be with the others, but they're so used to thinking of it as unclean. There's really a lot of education needed,' she added with a sigh.

'Oh, the poor thing.' How often had she felt like an outcast herself, because of her illegitimate birth? Instinctively she held out her arms to the little boy, and after a moment's hesitation he scrambled into her lap, hugging her fiercely. 'Oh, mind, you'll crush your flower,' she warned him gently, opening his fingers to take the delicate blossom from him. She handed it to the girl weaving her head-dress, who took it with a shy smile and inserted it carefully into the final place.

'Thank you,' murmured Sister Maria softly. 'That was very kind of you. There—they've finished now. And here's Father Ignatius.'

Rae rose quickly to her feet, setting the small boy down. Daniel had his back to her, flirting with the other girls, and again she had to suppress that uncomfortable pang of jealousy, reminding herself firmly that she had no claim on him at all.

The priest had changed from his white hospital coat into a flowing cassock, which swirled around his legs as he walked. The children ran to meet him, and he beamed down at them fondly. 'Steady now— it's far too hot for all this excitement.' He smiled at Rae. 'Well, now, are we all ready?' he enquired.

She nodded dumbly, flinching as she felt Daniel's hand on her elbow.

'Good, good. Well, this way—at least it should be a little cooler in the chapel.'

In a small procession they followed the priest through the exotic jungle of the garden. In any other circumstances Rae would have been enchanted by the riot of jewel-bright orchids and hibiscus, of sweetly fragrant frangipani, and shining pools filled with tall, delicate lotus flowers, but she was hardly even aware of her surroundings. She felt as if she were being escorted to her own execution.

Daniel glanced down at her, a sardonic smile curving his hard mouth. 'Those flowers in your hair look pretty,' he complimented her lightly. 'Very bridal.'

'Thank you,' she mumbled, subdued.

The chapel was set in a quiet corner of the mission compound, shaded by a stand of gracefully swaying casuarinas. Inside it was blissfully cool. The walls were panelled with wood, lovingly carved and gleaming from frequent polishing. A small altar, covered by an embroidered cloth, stood on a low dais before the rows of wooden pews, and everywhere there were flowers, seemingly hundreds of them, intricately woven into garlands and crosses, filling the air with their mingling perfumes. It would have been a perfect place to be married—if the marriage had been something more than an empty charade.

Sister Maria bustled over to the piano that stood to one side of the altar. She took her seat, lifting back the lace tablecloth that was draped over it and raising the cover to run her fingers over the yellowing ivory keys. And then, with a nod to the children, she began to play.

At once their piping voices rose into the vaulted ceiling, singing in fractured English—'All things bright and beautiful, All creatures great and small...'

Rae risked a quick glance up at Daniel. His eyes were as unreadable as ever, but his mouth still wore that faintly sardonic smile. He held out his hand, and reluctantly she placed hers in it, and let him lead her to the altar.

'Brother and sisters, we are gathered here together...' Father Ignatius, at least, was intent on conducting the ceremony as solemnly as if it *were* real. Rae lowered her eyes, wishing she could be anywhere on earth but here. 'Do thou, Daniel, take this woman to be thy lawfully wedded wife? Wilt thou love, honour and cherish her; for better or worse, for richer or poorer, in sickness and in health; and forsaking all others cleave thee only unto her, as long as ye both shall live?'

'I will.'

Rae's heart turned over. If only...

'Do thou, Raeleen...?'

'Do we have to go through all this?' she pleaded in a desperate whisper. 'Couldn't we just...?' The shocked look the priest gave her quelled her protest, and she hung her head again as he recited the vow. 'I will,' she murmured, her voice so faint that the quaver in it could barely be heard.

There was a little consternation when it came to the issue of a ring. Several of the girls quickly offered a loan of one of their pieces of cheap costume jewellery, but Daniel slid a plain gold signet ring from his own finger, and gave that to the priest.

'With this ring, I thee wed...'

It was far too big for her slender finger—she would have to be careful not to lose it. But of course she would be giving it back to him immediately after the ceremony.

'With my body I thee worship...'

Some compelling force made her lift her eyes to his, and her mouth felt suddenly dry. The memory of the way he had kissed her, the way his hands had caressed her, stirred in her brain—and the glint in his dark eyes told her that he was remembering too.

'And with all my worldly goods I thee endow.'

His mouth curved into a smile of cynical amusement. Was he thinking of that fifty rupals? Surely he didn't still believe that she had really intended to take it? No—he wouldn't be going through with all this if he thought that of her...would he?

'I now pronounce you man and wife. And that which God hath joined together, let no man put asunder.'

# CHAPTER FIVE

THE huge seven-four-seven lifted smoothly off the runway, and began to climb into the night sky. Rae gazed out of the window as the lights of Singapore receded below. It seemed almost impossible that it was only three days since they had landed here— in those three days her whole world had been turned upside down.

She shifted awkwardly in her seat—not that she could complain about the standard of comfort, she reflected wryly. It was just that plain Miss Rae Dillon belonged downstairs in the crowded economy class with her friends, not here in the pampered luxury of the first-class cabin.

But Daniel had insisted that she travel with him— as his wife, he had pointed out, it would look strange if they travelled separately. She slanted a covert look at the man sitting beside her. It hadn't taken her long to realise that there were distinct advantages to being Lady Amory.

For a start, Sir George's mocking prediction had proved to be one hundred per cent accurate. After waving an affectionate goodbye to Father Ignatius and Sister Maria, they had driven straight back to the police station, and one short, crisp interview later she had been free to go, all charges against her hurriedly dropped and one senior police officer severely embarrassed. Within a few hours they had all been on a plane to Singapore.

And there the talisman had worked again. With all flights for the next two days apparently fully booked, six seats had been somehow conjured out of nowhere for Lord Amory's party. The airline staff couldn't have been more helpful.

She glanced down at her left hand. There was no ring there now to mark her temporary status—it was back on Daniel's little finger. All she had to remember that strange ceremony by was a fading lotus flower, carefully pressed between the pages of her diary.

It hadn't been the wedding she had dreamed for herself. She should have been dressed in white, with lace and a veil, not cream-coloured cotton trousers. And it should have been the little parish church round the corner from where her mother lived, where she had gone to Sunday School, not some tiny mission chapel on the other side of the world. And her mother should have been there.

Perhaps the simplest thing to do would be not to even tell her mother about what had happened, at least not until it was some distant memory to laugh about together. She had had enough worries in her life, without the added burden of this.

Cautiously she slanted another sideways glance up at Daniel. He had opened his briefcase as soon as they had been settled on the plane, and taken out some important-looking papers, and, with a polite word of apology to her, as if he thought she had been expecting him to keep her entertained, he had begun to read them.

It was odd to think that this virtual stranger was her husband. In the inside pocket of that well-cut jacket was a marriage licence with their two names on it. That had been an awkward moment, signing the register, she recalled with a twinge of embarrassment. Father Ignatius had had difficulty fitting in all the fine aristocratic names of Daniel's late father in the small space provided—they had been laughing over it.

And then he had looked up at her in innocent expectation, waiting for her to supply the necessary details. She hadn't been able to think of an elegant way of phrasing it, so she had just stated bluntly, 'I haven't got a father—I'm illegitimate.' That had gone down like a lead balloon.

The plane levelled out, and the seatbelt light went off, and a moment later the cabin steward came to offer them champagne before dinner. Daniel declined, favouring a glass of mineral water, but Rae accepted, and sipped it as she gazed out of the window at the acres of darkness below.

'Are you all right?' Daniel asked, as formally as if he had been a stranger.

'Yes, of course I am.' She had set her face into a cool mask as she turned back to him, hiding all the turmoil of emotions inside her. 'Why shouldn't I be?'

'No particular reason,' he acknowledged drily. 'I just wondered if you were tired, that's all.'

'A little,' she conceded, not smiling. 'It's been rather a long day.'

'Yes, it has.'

If his dark eyes were searching hers for some give-away sign that she was bothered what he was thinking, she was careful to ensure that he couldn't get past her guard. Now that she was his wife, however temporarily, it was going to be harder than ever to resist the kind of demands she knew he wanted to make on her. Her only defence would be to keep him at arm's length—if he should once suspect her weakness, she would be lost.

He smiled wryly. 'You know, at the risk of sounding appallingly conceited, I have to say that quite a lot of women would probably have been quite pleased at the prospect of marrying me,' he remarked. 'You seem to be reacting as if it's the worst disaster that's ever befallen you.'

Rae had to fight to maintain her composed façade—he was far too shrewd to be easy to deceive. 'Am I?' she managed to respond, injecting a measurable degree of indifference into her voice. 'I'm sorry—of course I'm very grateful to you for helping me out. I just wish it could have been some other way—it's going to be such a drag, sorting out the annulment and all that. Still...' she shrugged her slim shoulders in a dismissive gesture '...I suppose it can't be helped.'

His eyes took on a cynical glint. 'We can leave all that to my lawyers,' he said. 'You and I need only think about the—er—more pleasurable aspects of our acquaintance.'

His meaning was unmistakable, and her heart began to flutter alarmingly. But she managed to keep her voice commendably cool as she enquired, 'Don't you think that might rather interfere with the legal disentanglements?'

'No—why should it?' he countered, an inflexion of sardonic humour in his voice.

'Well, as I understand it, the simplest grounds for the annulment will be . . . non-consummation.'

'Yes?'

'I suppose we'll have to sign sworn statements or something?'

'I don't know—one would assume so,' he conceded.

'Then if we . . . lied, it would mean we were committing perjury,' she went on, her voice carefully ironed of any trace of emotion. 'I don't think we ought to do that.'

He laughed softly. 'Such scruples,' he taunted. 'You surprise me. Very well, then, we'll wait until after Lythgoe has sorted everything out.'

'And then?' She couldn't quite suppress the quaver in her voice.

'And then . . .' He smiled slowly, leaning towards her, and lifted his hand to trace one tantalising fingertip along the full curve of her lower lip. 'And then we can do whatever we like.' His voice was so low that it seemed to vibrate through her skin instead of her hearing, like the deepest notes of a cello. She stared up at him, held captive by those mesmerising dark eyes, drowning in them——

'Would you like duck or lobster, *madame*?'

She blinked, looking up, startled, as the cabin steward hovered over the trolley with a fine china dinner-plate in his hand, waiting for her to make her selection. 'Oh . . . I'll have . . . the duck, please,' she choked out, hoping that he would think her hectic colour was due to the heat in the cabin.

Evidently he did, for he leaned over and adjusted the air-conditioning vent above her seat, checking that it was working. 'Is that better, *madame*?' he asked politely.

'Yes . . . thank you,' she mumbled, unwrapping her silver knife and fork from the fine linen napkin—no disposable plastic and paper here. She had been grateful for the interruption—that conversation had been getting seriously out of hand!

The food was delicious, but she couldn't enjoy it. She had tried to tell Daniel how she felt, and he had only mocked her. And he still believed that after the marriage was annulled she would happily become his mistress—even if he kept his promise to wait that long! From the very first he hadn't troubled to hide his powerful sexual interest in her— and she knew that she was all too vulnerable.

She could sense him watching her now as she nervously pushed the food around on her plate. Somehow she managed to force herself to fork a little of the duck into her mouth. It was exquisitely cooked, so tender that it seemed to almost melt on her tongue, but it could have been sulphur and ashes for all the impression it made on her appetite.

'What's wrong?' Daniel enquired, slanting her a mocking look. 'You don't seem to be enjoying your dinner.'

'Oh, no, it's...very nice,' she responded quickly. 'It's as good as a restaurant—a bit different to what you get dished up downstairs!'

He laughed softly. 'Stick with me, kid, and you can travel first class all the time.'

She laughed too, but shook her head. 'I'm not that mercenary.'

He regarded her thoughtfully. 'Maybe you're not,' he agreed, but there was a trace of cynical doubt in his voice. 'You're certainly trying to give that impression at the moment, anyway. Why, I wonder? Are you hoping to lure me into losing my head over you, so that I'm tempted to turn this marriage into a permanent arrangement?'

'Of course not!' Her protest was much too sharp, and he smiled in sardonic amusement.

'You're a very good little actress,' he taunted. 'But not quite good enough. I didn't come down in the last shower of rain. I want you, but I've no intention of letting you trap me. So if you've got any tricks planned, you can just forget about them right now.'

She couldn't answer him—maybe she deserved that he should have such a low opinion of her, but that didn't stop it hurting. Somehow she managed to swallow a few more bites of her meal before the cabin steward came round to offer dessert. There was a choice of profiteroles or crème brûlée, but she refused both, and, clipping her flight-table up out of the way, she reclined her seat. Settling under the soft vicuña blanket she had been given, she closed her eyes and pretended to be asleep.

By the time they had landed at Gatwick, Rae was too tired to care about anything. After nearly fifteen hours in the air, followed by a wait of several hours in Paris for a flight to London, she felt totally disorientated, bewildered by the seven hours' time loss, dizzy from an illusory sensation of continuing motion.

Like a zombie she followed Daniel through passport control and Customs, just grateful for his strong, competent presence to take care of everything for her, relieving her of the necessity to tax her exhausted brain at all. Only Mel was with them—the plane had been full, so the other three girls had had to take a slightly later flight to Heathrow, from where they would go straight to Liz's mother's house in Hounslow where they were going to stay.

Daniel glanced down at her, frowning slightly at the pallor of her cheeks. 'Don't worry, my car will be here,' he told her. 'You can sleep as soon as we get home.'

She nodded vaguely; it was several seconds before his words came into focus in her brain. 'Wait...I'm not going home with you,' she protested, catching his arm as he wheeled their luggage trolley across the arrivals hall towards the exit.

'Where else do you think you're going to go?' he enquired with calm patience.

'I . . .' She couldn't think—jet lag had turned her brain to cotton wool.

'That's a point,' put in Mel, looking anxious. 'Where *are* we going to stay?'

All Rae knew was that she couldn't stay with Daniel. 'Oh, we'll find somewhere,' she insisted weakly. 'A hotel or something. . .'

'We can't afford a hotel,' Mel pointed out, the strain of concentration wrinkling her brow. 'It's a nuisance we gave up our flat—we can't go back there now. I suppose we could give Gerry a ring—oh, no, he's doing a summer show in Blackpool.'

'Then there's no argument,' concluded Daniel firmly. 'Mel, you're very welcome to come too, until you're able to find somewhere else.'

'Oh, *could* I?' exclaimed Mel, innocently unaware of the reason why Rae was frantically shaking her head. 'Thank you ever so much—that would be brilliant. It wouldn't be for long, I promise—I'll start looking for a flat tomorrow.'

Rae knew she ought to argue, but her head ached with weariness at the thought. After all, it would be just for this one night—tomorrow she and Mel would find somewhere else.

She hadn't quite taken in what Daniel had said about his car being there—she had assumed that he had left it in one of the vast car parks surrounding the airport. It was something of a surprise when a sleek dark-blue Rolls-Royce drew up to the kerb beside them, and a young chauffeur got out.

His eyes flickered over the two weary girls, registering curiosity. 'Good trip, sir?' he enquired of Daniel, his voice hinting for at least an introduction.

'Interesting,' responded Daniel drily. 'Put all the luggage in the boot, Gibson.'

'Yes, sir.' The young man was clearly intrigued, but knew that he was going to have to wait a little longer for any explanation of these unexpected guests. In the meantime, he wasn't loath to signal his approval of his boss's taste.

As Rae settled in a corner of the back seat, she spared a wry wish that she hadn't been so tired and could have better appreciated her first-ever ride in a Rolls-Royce. The warm leather upholstery was as soft as a cloud, and as the engine purred into life she closed her eyes and drifted away into the comfort of sleep.

Daylight was filtering through a dark-green curtain. Rae turned on the pillow, puzzled by a striped pillow and a Japanese-patterned quilt-cover that matched the curtains. She was in a wide double bed, and someone else had slept in the other half of it.

Slowly the jumbled puzzle of dreams resolved itself into a memory of reality, and she sat up sharply. She was in her underwear—her clothes were on a chair beside the bed. Vaguely she recalled dumping them there as she had peeled them off—though not folding them so tidily as they were now.

Other images, like dim snatches of film, came into her mind. A quiet street, reeking of discreet prosperity—somewhere in Mayfair or Belgravia, she would guess. A terrace of tall grey Georgian houses, with basements guarded by wrought-iron railings, and gracious stone porches. Four wide steps, leading up to a gleaming front door.

There was a butler, she remembered now, formally polite but as pent with curiosity as the chauffeur. He had brought them coffee and sandwiches in a drawing-room of magnificent proportions, luxuriously furnished with cream upholstery and walnut tables. She had managed to eat only one sandwich, though they were delicious—cottage cheese, and cucumber with the rind trimmed off.

Then Daniel had brought them both upstairs, showing Mel into a charming blue chintz room further along the corridor, and leading her in here. She had been too tired to mumble more than a token protest, but if anything had happened after her head had hit the pillow she wasn't aware of it; she must have already been asleep.

No—nothing *had* happened. She would certainly know if... Biting her lip, she scrambled out of bed and reached for her clothes. Her bag, not opened since she had claimed it from the police station in Kahyangan, was on the floor. There must be a bathroom somewhere...?

There were three doors to choose from. One opened on to the corridor, and another into a very large walk-in cupboard stocked with expensive suits and tailored shirts and casual clothes of the best quality. Behind the third she found the bathroom, a pragmatic combination of modern convenience and thirties elegance.

There was no lock on the door, so she couldn't savour the luxury of the claw-footed bathtub; instead she had to make do with a rapid slick-wash, then dressed quickly and brushed out the tangles from her hair, tossing it back around her shoulders with a shake of her head.

She hadn't adjusted her watch back to English time, but a quick calculation told her that it was almost midday; that long sleep had done a great deal to cure the effects of a double dose of jet lag. She felt almost human again. And now there could be no excuse not to take over control of her own life again. The first thing to do was find Mel.

Her friend was still asleep, half buried beneath a pale blue quilt, her snuffling snores stirring the strands of golden hair tumbled across her face. It seemed almost a shame to wake her, but Rae knew she had to be ruthless. 'Mel?' She shook her shoulder firmly. 'Come on, wake up. It's nearly lunchtime.'

'Mmm?' Like a warm hamster, Mel burrowed into the pillow, and then reluctantly opened her eyes. 'What is it?' she mumbled.

'Time to get up,' insisted Rae, feeling a pang of guilt for waking her.

'Oooh.' Mel rolled over, and pulled the quilt up around her ear again, but Rae shook her once more, determined. Mel turned, her eyes clearing of sleep, and lifted herself up on one elbow. 'All right,' she conceded. 'Hey, just look at this.' She gazed around

the room in awe. 'You could be on to a good thing
here, kid, if you play your cards right!'

'Don't be silly,' Rae silenced her warningly.
'Come on, get up and pack your things. We have
to find somewhere else to go.'

'Why?' Mel blinked at her in sympathetic
concern. 'Have you had a row with him already?'

'No—I haven't even seen him this morning. But
I don't want to stay here a minute longer than I
have to.'

Mel clambered out of bed, and reached for the
froth of pink chiffon she had dropped on the carpet.
'Wait a minute while I find my contact lenses,' she
pleaded. 'I don't see why we have to go—Danny
said we could stay till we found somewhere else,
and we haven't even started looking yet.'

'No, but we're going to start right now,' Rae asserted, fishing the white plastic case that held her
friend's contact lenses out from the clutter of make-
up in the floral plastic toilet-bag on the dressing-
table.

Mel shrugged. 'All right—but it's not going to
be that easy. Besides, we don't have much money,
and they always want a deposit, even for something
the size of a shoe-box with the bathroom down three
flights of stairs.'

'I know. But we have to find something.'

'Any chance of getting something to eat first?'
Mel enquired hopefully. 'I'm starving.'

Rae would have preferred not to wait for lunch,
but as she was slipping back to her own room she
almost collided with the butler, who was evidently

coming to look for them. 'Ah, you're awake, madam,' he greeted her with lofty dignity. 'Lord Amory has gone to his office, I'm afraid, but he asked me to see that you have everything you need. I've prepared some lunch—shall I serve it now?'

'Oh...thank you,' agreed Rae uncertainly.

'I've set a table in the morning-room—to the left at the bottom of the stairs. Whenever you're ready...?'

Five minutes later, the two girls crept downstairs like a pair of errant schoolgirls, both a little over-awed by the magnificence of the marble-floored hall, the medieval oak settle against the wall, the fine chandeliers suspended from the high ceiling.

'Oh, boy!' whispered Mel, gazing around. 'I don't know why you're so keen to do a bunk—we could never afford a pad like this in a million years!'

'Ssh!' whispered Rae warningly, casting an anxious glance over her shoulder in case the butler should be within earshot.

The morning-room was bigger than the bedsit they had shared before their ill-fated trip to Singapore. Bronze-green velvet swag curtains framed the two tall windows that overlooked the street, and the furniture had the look of having been collected over several generations. A round pedestal-legged table between the windows had been set for two, and Rae lifted the cover to find a salad, and a cheese-board stocked with six varieties of cheese.

'Mmm.' Mel sat down, and examined her plate closely. 'There's walnuts in this, and that looks like avocado. And that fancy curly lettuce stuff—I've had that before.' She picked up her knife and fork, and tucked in hungrily. 'Try it,' she invited to Rae. 'It's really nice.'

Rae was quite sure that it was, but she wasn't very happy about eating it. She would have preferred to have popped into a McDonald's somewhere—though at the moment every penny counted. They would *have* to find a place today. Anything would do.

But by eight o'clock that evening, footsore and weary, she had to concede defeat. Mel had been sulking for the past three hours, and now she was in full-scale rebellion.

'That's it!' she declared, perching somewhat precariously on a shop window-sill and taking off one shoe to examine her reddened toes. 'I've had enough—why can't we go home?'

'You shouldn't have worn those shoes,' Rae advised her with strained patience. 'You knew we'd have to do a lot of walking.'

Mel pouted. 'We could have got a taxi...'

'And waste money on fares when we're going to need it all to pay a deposit?'

'Well, we aren't going to have to pay a deposit, because we haven't got a flat,' Mel pointed out sulkily. 'So we can get a taxi home. And it's no good looking in the paper again. We've been to every single agency and rung every single advert, and there's absolutely nothing at all, not unless we happened to have about ten grand sloshing around. We won't find anything in a month of Sundays.'

Rae sank down beside her, dispirited. 'But we have to find somewhere,' she protested miserably. 'We can't stay where we are indefinitely.'

'I don't get it,' probed Mel. 'I thought you really liked him. You've got to admit, he's as tasty as they come.'

'Oh, yes, he's ... very attractive,' conceded Rae a little stiffly. 'But ... Oh, you must see it, Mel. I can't stay—the longer I stay the more complicated it's going to get. He's going to expect ... that I'll sleep with him.'

'I thought you were,' remarked Mel innocently.

'Of course I'm not!' Rae protested, her cheeks scarlet.

'Well, you *are* married to him,' Mel pointed out.

'Yes, but that was just a ... a convenience, a way of getting out of trouble with the police so I could come home. It wasn't meant to be a proper marriage.'

'But he fancies you,' Mel asserted. 'Anyone can see that.'

Rae sighed wistfully. 'I know—but it's only... wanting to get me into bed. He doesn't want to be married to me.'

'You really *do* like him, don't you?' asked Mel, her voice soft with sympathy.

Rae blinked back the tears that had welled into her eyes. 'Yes, I do,' she whispered.

Mel patted her hand. 'All right—we'll find ourselves another place to stay somehow. Come on—

keep your chin up. Tomorrow's a whole new day, and there must be *one* teeny tiny flat for us somewhere in this vast metropolis.' She waved her hand in an expansive gesture. 'Ooh—there's a taxi. Come on, quick—don't argue. I'm paying.'

It was Daniel himself who opened the front door for them. He smiled in sympathy when he saw how wearily they dragged themselves into the house. 'You look exhausted,' he remarked. 'Where have you been?'

'Flat-hunting,' supplied Mel, the tightness in her voice conveying graphically all the setbacks and disappointments of the day.

'Ah. Well, I expect you'd like to have a wash, and then dinner will be ready,' he told them.

Rae looked up at him in surprise. 'Haven't you eaten? You didn't wait for us?' she asked anxiously.

He laughed, and shook his head. 'I've only just come in myself,' he assured her. 'After being away from my desk for over a week, there was rather a lot awaiting my attention.'

'Oh . . .'

He caught her hand, detaining her as she moved to follow Mel up the stairs. 'Why are *you* looking for a flat?' he enquired softly, drawing her towards him. 'You're staying right here.'

He slid his hand into her hair to cradle her skull, and she knew that he was going to kiss her. Instantly she stiffened in resistance, holding herself away from him. A question lit in his dark eyes. 'I . . . Not at the moment,' she managed to stumble.

'I . . . I want to change, and have a quick wash. I haven't eaten since lunchtime.'

'All right.' He looked suspicious, but he let her go, and she fled upstairs to the bedroom she had shared with him the night before.

It was a large room, but the big double bed seemed to dominate it. She gazed at it in wide-eyed apprehension, biting her lip. Tonight, Daniel would be expecting her to share it with him again. She had tried to tell him on the plane that she wasn't going to sleep with him, but it had been a feeble attempt, and she had rather undermined it by the ease with which she had taken off her clothes and fallen into bed with him last night.

With a small twinge of guilt she remembered that she had been almost relieved that she was too tired to argue, as if that absolved her of any responsibility for what she had assumed was going to happen. But she had no such convenient excuse tonight.

Dinner would have been a very strained meal if it hadn't been for Mel's lively presence. She burbled away happily, telling Daniel all about their unsuccessful afternoon's flat-hunting, apparently totally oblivious to any sign of tension between the two other occupants of the table.

Rae could only pick at her meal, though the beef tournedos were tender enough to melt in her mouth. Over and over she was rehearsing in her mind the forthcoming confrontation with Daniel, trying to find the words to explain her position, but all she was succeeding in doing was making herself feel more nervous than ever.

She was watching him covertly from beneath her lashes, studying every line of that hard-boned, handsome face, searching for some clue to how he would react to her refusal to do as he wanted. She could well imagine that he wouldn't be used to having a woman resist him. A small shiver ran through her. What would he do? She would probably be getting off lightly if he threw her out into the street in the middle of the night.

'Are you cold?' he asked, turning to her so suddenly that her heart thumped in alarm.

'Oh... No.' She shook her head.

'You haven't eaten much—aren't you hungry?'

'No, I...I think I've gone past it,' she mumbled.

'Well, perhaps you'll be able to manage something later,' he suggested. 'We might as well have coffee in the drawing-room. Do you want some?'

'Er—yes, please.'

'I think I'll turn in,' announced Mel with a wide yawn. 'I'm bushed!'

Rae turned to her in horror. She couldn't leave her on her own with him, not yet! She wasn't ready, she hadn't worked out what to say...! 'Oh, just stay and have some coffee first,' she pleaded, her eyes signalling a frantic message. But Mel had never been very good at picking up unspoken hints, however heavily they were put.

'No—I don't feel like any really,' she demurred. 'I just want to tuck down in bed—I'm not really over that jet lag yet, and we walked so far today.

G'night, sleep tight, mind the fleas don't bite.' Yawning again, she rose to her feet, and wove out of the door.

Daniel was smiling, amused by Mel's sleepy farewell, but as he turned to Rae the dark look of intent in his eyes chilled her to the bone. 'Well,' he remarked, reaching for her hand. 'Shall we adjourn to the drawing-room, or shall we go straight up to bed too?'

'The—er—the drawing-room,' she managed, swallowing hard.

A flicker of sardonic humour crossed his hard mouth; he had recognised her resistance, and he was going to enjoy breaking it down.

He drew her to her feet, and led her across the hall to the room where they had had their coffee the night before. He settled her on a large, comfortable settee, and sat down beside her as the butler brought in a silver tray bearing two fine white china cups and a silver pot. 'Thank you, Elliot— that will be all now,' he said.

As the door closed behind the butler, leaving them alone together, Rae eased herself slightly away from him. 'Cream and sugar?' she enquired, her voice sounding strained even to her own ears.

'No sugar.'

As she poured the coffee she could feel those dark eyes resting on her, and it was impossible to keep her hand steady. She managed a light laugh. 'Sorry,' she mumbled, apologising for the slop of coffee in the saucer as she handed it to him. 'The pot's rather heavy.'

He smiled, one of those lingering caressing smiles that seemed to melt her bones. 'You look tired,' he remarked softly.

'Yes, I am, rather,' she responded, over-bright. 'Like Mel, I'm not really over the jet lag yet. How do you manage? It doesn't seem to have affected you.'

'I'm used to it.'

'Oh . . . You must travel quite a lot?'

'Yes, I do. My bank has interests all over the world.'

She nodded, glad that the conversation was flowing so easily on such neutral lines. 'Which bank do you work for?' she asked.

A flicker of sardonic amusement curved his hard mouth. 'Amory Morgan and Ross,' he told her.

Her eyes widened. 'Oh. You mean . . . it really is "your" bank?' She ought to have known. Just how rich, how powerful, was he?

'I don't own all of it,' he responded, smiling grimly. 'I have eighteen per cent of the shares, and I'm the chairman.'

'Only eighteen per cent?' She shrugged her slim shoulders, trying to make a joke of it. 'And I thought you were a millionaire.'

'Oh, I am.' He put down his cup, and drew her inexorably into his arms. 'The bank's capitalised at over seventy million pounds. And then I own land—several hundred acres in Northamptonshire, a few square miles of Scotland, as well as some rather well-placed holdings here in London. Need I go on?'

She gazed up into his eyes, knowing that she was falling helplessly under their hypnotic spell once again, try as she might to resist. His fingers were laced in her hair, and she knew that she wasn't going to be able to escape. She should have said something sooner...

'Or do you think that will be sufficient to overcome your stout reluctance to stay in my house?'

She tried to utter some word of protest, but she was silenced as his mouth claimed hers in an insistent demand that she didn't know how to withstand. His tongue swept deep into the sweet, moist valley of her mouth, swirling languorously over the sensitive membranes within, and she could do nothing to stop him as he began to unfasten the buttons down the front of her cheap cotton blouse, one by one.

He brushed the fabric back, to find that she was still wearing the silk bra he had bought her in the hotel in Kahyangan. 'Mmm—I was looking forward to seeing you in this,' he murmured, his voice soft and husky as he ran his fingertip lightly around the delicate lace edging. 'Very fetching.'

Her breasts were aching for his touch, and with a blush of shame she knew that the tender nipples were ripening beneath his lingering gaze, treacherously betraying her response. That idle fingertip circled slowly over the firm swell, tantalising her. Weakly her mind struggled to retain its grip on sanity, but she was losing the battle: he was subduing her will with his smooth seduction.

'That's better,' he taunted, his eyes mocking her. 'At least you're being honest now—the virginal innocent you try to play sometimes is hardly believable, you know. Besides, I prefer you just the way you are—willing and wanton and utterly bewitching.'

'No...I...' But as his thumb brushed lightly over the hard, sensitised bud of her nipple she forgot what she had been going to say, and it came out instead as a low, sensuous moan.

He chuckled with triumphant laughter, and his mouth brushed hers again, gentle but insistent, coaxing apart her lips with a tempting persuasion that she could not resist. He was luring her out of her depth, his tongue plundering deep into her mouth, warning her of a possessive demand that would brook no opposition.

His hand had eased the filmy silk of her bra out of the way, and was caressing her naked breasts, rolling the exquisitely sensitive buds of her nipples beneath his palm, teasingly pinching them between his fingers, reducing her to a state of helpless abandon.

'Mmm—you could tempt a man to far worse than perjury,' he growled, his kisses swirling into the sensitive shell of her ear. 'I can hardly believe I've been to bed with you twice, and yet I've never touched you like this. How have we managed to wait so long? Two whole days and two whole nights...'

His hot mouth trailed down the long, sensitive column of her throat, sending a shivering response through her, and her head tipped back into the crook of his arm. She could hear her own breathing, ragged and impeded, hear the racing beat of her heart. She shouldn't be letting this happen, she shouldn't . . .

The sinuous lap of his tongue around one tender pink nipple swirled a dart of fire into her brain, and as he took the succulent bud deep into his mouth and began to suckle with a hungry rhythm she could only surrender herself to the desire that was drowning her. She loved him, and whatever he wanted from her she would give.

Somewhere in the house a telephone was ringing insistently, but neither of them took any notice of it. They were lost in the dark world of sensuous pleasure that had engulfed them both, and nothing else was real . . .

# CHAPTER SIX

IT WAS only when someone began to rap loudly on the door of the drawing-room that Daniel lifted his head. 'What is it?' he demanded, his voice raw with impatience.

The door opened a few discreet inches, and Rae heard the butler clear his throat. 'I'm very sorry sir, but it's Mr Cunningham on the line from Canada,' he announced. 'There's been some kind of problem at the plant—he says he has to speak to you at once.'

'Damn! All right, Elliott—I'm coming.' Reluctantly he rose to his feet, and with a wry smile down at Rae he pulled the front of her blouse over to cover her naked breasts. 'I won't be long,' he murmured huskily. 'Keep it warm for me.'

He went out, leaving her struggling to grasp at the scattered threads of her sanity. What had happened to all her good intentions? One touch, one kiss from him and they had melted away like April snow. If that telephone call hadn't interrupted them ...

And now what was she going to do? In a moment he would be back, and then ... She was shamed to admit that she didn't have the strength to resist him any further. All she wanted was to be back in those strong arms, to feel that lean, hard body against hers, to yield to every demanding caress...

Daniel was gone for several minutes. She sat up sharply as he came back into the room, a swift tug of concern snatching at her heart as she saw his darkly worried frown. 'Is there something wrong?' she asked anxiously.

He nodded. 'The bank owns a chemicals plant in British Columbia. There's been an explosion...'

She gasped. 'Oh, dear—was anyone killed?'

'Not so far as we know—everyone seems to be accounted for. We were very lucky. But there's a serious threat of environmental pollution—it could have a disastrous effect on the local rivers. I have to go out there right away.'

'Oh...' Her mind spun in a vortex of confusion. This was her release from the trap of fate that had been dragging her towards her own destruction— but she wasn't sure that she wanted to be free.

He came across and leaned over the back of the settee, tilting her head back so that she was gazing up at him. 'I hate to leave you—just when it was getting interesting,' he murmured. His mouth brushed across hers—upside down—and he laughed smokily. 'Damn British Columbia,' he growled, moving round to sit on the arm of the settee beside her and lifting her into his arms. 'Let them look out for their own rivers.'

His kiss plundered deep into the sweet, defenceless valley of her mouth, savouring every secret corner. She surrendered totally, forgetting all her reservations. She longed for the caress of his hand moulding her ripe breast, longed to feel his warm, hard body against hers . . .

But with a low groan he let her go. 'Oh, if only it were that easy,' he sighed. 'But I have to go. I'll get back as soon as I can.'

Rae opened her eyes, an ice-cold chill blowing through her as he left her. She could hear him calling for his butler as he ran up the stairs. How easily he could switch on and off, she reflected bitterly. He had pretended for a moment that he couldn't bear to leave her, and she—fool!—had almost believed him.

But the demands of his bank had taken priority, and he had just walked away from her, leaving her aching with unfulfilled desires. And if she were stupid enough to succumb to his practised seduction, that was how it would always be. He wanted her, but he would never allow that to intrude on the rest of his life—she would be relegated to a small corner marked 'sex', and that would be her sole function in his life.

She heard his coming downstairs again, and for a moment she stayed where she was, mutinously refusing to go and say goodbye to him. But she couldn't bear to let him go without seeing him one last time—and this time she knew it must be the last time. She wouldn't be here when he got back.

He was in the hall, shrugging into the jacket of his business suit, his well-travelled leather suitcase at his feet. He looked up as she opened the door, a smile of remembered intimacy in his eyes. He reached out, and drew her into his arms. 'I have to be there,' he said, his voice low and coaxing. 'There are casualties, though it doesn't look as if anyone's been seriously hurt, and with this risk of damage to the local ecology... It wouldn't do just to leave it to the plant manager. The bank is responsible.'

She nodded, not able to speak, and let her forehead rest against his wide shoulder, breathing in the subtle male muskiness of his skin. She couldn't even tell him of her plans to leave—if he should try to persuade her to stay, she didn't think she would be able to refuse him.

He turned his head to kiss the sensitive hollow behind her ear, nuzzling against her until she lifted her face to his, offering her mouth for his kiss. With gentle possessiveness he accepted the invitation, his caressing hand moving again to her breast as if he wanted to engrave her soft shape on his memory and take it with him.

But at long last he lifted his head, and reluctantly put her away from him. 'I *have* to go,' he insisted, his voice husky with the effort of suppressing the powerful male desire she could sense in him. 'I'll be back as soon as I can.' And then he was gone, the butler opening the door for him, the chauffeur waiting on the top step to take his suitcase.

Rae woke alone again in the big double bed; but this time there was no rumpled pillow beside her, and the smell of Daniel's body had almost faded from the sheets. A glance at her watch told her that it was barely seven in the morning, and it had been after four o'clock when she had finally stopped tossing and turning. But she knew she wouldn't sleep any more now, so she swung out of bed, and padded into the luxurious bathroom to run herself a tub of steaming foam-laced water.

By the time she got downstairs the morning papers had arrived, and she sat on the bottom stair, poring over them for any information about the accident in Canada. Not all of them had picked it up, and those that had didn't seem to have much information—just a few lines about reports of an explosion at a British-owned factory, and that Lord Amory was expected to arrive as soon as possible to see for himself what needed to be done to prevent a major environmental catastrophe.

The ring of the telephone startled her, and she picked it up without thinking—it could be Daniel, calling to let her know how things were going. 'Hello?'

A voice she didn't recognise said, 'Good morning—sorry to trouble you so early. Could I speak to Lord Amory, please?'

'Oh...' A wave of disappointment swept through her. 'I'm sorry, he isn't here at present. There's been an explosion at one of his factories in Canada, and he's had to fly out there straight away.'

'Ah, yes. And...who is that speaking?' the voice enquired.

'Oh, I'm...just a friend,' she responded uncertainly.

'Not his housekeeper?'

'No. He hasn't got a housekeeper—at least, I don't think so. Would you like to speak to his butler? I'm not sure if he's up yet...'

'No, it's all right. Actually, you might be the very person I was hoping to speak to. Is that Raeleen?'

She stared at the telephone in shock. 'How did you know my name?'

He laughed smugly. 'So it *is* Raeleen. I understand that you're actually rather more than a friend of Lord Amory, isn't that so?'

'Who told you? Who is that?'

'My name's Bob Stirling, from the *Daily Mercury*. We've picked up a story that you and Lord Amory were secretly married a few days ago on some tropical island paradise in the Pacific. Is it true? Would you like to tell me how you met him?'

'No!' Her hand was shaking. How on earth had the newspapers found out so quickly? 'You can't print that!'

'Are you telling me that it isn't true—you aren't married to him?'

'Yes, I am, but... How did you find out about it? We aren't—I mean, it isn't... It wasn't a proper marriage. It was only——' She bit her lip, suddenly realising that she ought to be very careful what she said—it could so easily be twisted around and made to sound completely different. 'I'm sorry, I can't tell you anything,' she asserted firmly.

'You know he's listed as the second most eligible bachelor in the country?' the voice persisted, taunting now. 'How did you manage to catch him?'

'I didn't catch him! I . . .'

'Could you tell me a little bit about yourself? For the record. How old you are? Where you were born, what sort of work you were doing before you were married?'

'No, I couldn't,' she blurted, appalled. 'I don't want to speak to you at all. Goodbye!' She slammed the telephone down, and sat staring at it, trembling. It started ringing again almost at once, and she picked it up gingerly, as if afraid that it would give her an electric shock.

The same voice again. 'We're going with the story for tomorrow's edition,' he said. 'Do you want to add any comment?'

'No, I don't!' she shouted, close to tears. 'And don't call me again!' She slammed the receiver down again.

'Rac?' Mel's blonde head appeared above her, leaning over the banisters. 'What is it? What's going on?'

'The papers!' she wailed in distress. 'Someone's told them about me and Daniel.'

'But no one knows about it yet except us, and you told us not to tell anyone. It wouldn't have been Liz or Angie or Cathy, and it certainly wasn't me.'

'I don't know who it could have been,' sighed Rae. 'Lady Havering? She wasn't too pleased about it, and it's just the sort of catty thing she would do. Or maybe they just got it from the airline or something—somebody who noticed our names on the passenger list, and thought they might make a few quid by selling the information to the Press.'

'Oh, dear.' Mel had come down to sit on the stairs beside her. 'Does Danny know about it yet?'

'No—he's gone to Canada.'

'Canada?'

'There's been some sort of accident at a factory out there,' Rae explained with a vague gesture of her hand. 'He had to go and sort it out, and just sort of *be* there—I suppose it's the sort of thing that could bring bad publicity to the bank if they don't handle it very carefully.'

'So could this,' mused Mel, echoing Rae's own thoughts. 'He isn't going to like it. Do you suppose he could sue them?'

'No—what for? It's only the truth—though we haven't seen what they're going to print yet.' She caught her bottom lip between her teeth and began to chew on it in her agitation. 'Anyway, one thing's for certain—by hook or by crook we have to find ourselves somewhere else to go. We can't stay here— that would only make things worse than ever.'

Mel nodded, though there was a wistful look in her blue eyes. 'Yes, I suppose so,' she conceded reluctantly. 'Though I must say I'll be sorry to leave here—I've never lived in such a super place in my whole life.'

They didn't manage to find a flat, but on the one-eight-five bus to Catford they met an old friend, who, on hearing of their desperation, offered to put them up for a couple of weeks if they didn't mind sleeping on the floor. They accepted with alacrity, and hurried back to the house in Belgravia to collect their things.

They had just reached the front door when two men jumped out of a car parked at the kerb. 'Rae?' one of them called.

'Yes?' Too late she realised that the other had a camera. She turned her back quickly, trying to hunch her head inside the collar of her coat, but he had already fired off several shots. Mel rapped sharply on the front door, and it opened almost at once. The two girls fell inside, to the astonishment of the lofty butler.

'Ah—you're home, miss,' he greeted her, his bland professionalism masking whatever he was thinking. 'Lady Amory is here to see you—she's waiting in the drawing-room.'

'Oh, lord!' muttered Rae, biting her lip. 'That's put the cat among the pigeons!'

She would have at least liked to have had a chance to tidy herself up a little before she had to face the dragon, but at that moment an imperious voice called from the drawing-room, 'Elliot? If that is the—er—young woman, kindly show her in at once.'

Mel's eyes widened in awe, and she slanted her friend a glance of heartfelt sympathy as she crept away upstairs. Rae managed a swift glance in the gilded mirror in the hall, enough to pull her jacket straight and to realise that her hair was badly in need of a brush, before the butler had opened the door for her and she was forced to step into the room.

The woman seated in the high-backed Queen Anne chair was unmistakably Daniel's mother—she had the same autocratic features, the same ruthless cast of jaw. She would have been about sixty, and she certainly wouldn't ever have deigned to disguise the silver in her dark hair, which was arranged with formidable control in crisp waves.

Rae found herself the subject of a long, cool gaze, assessing her with a hauteur that made Lady Havering seem almost friendly by comparison. 'So... You are the young woman whom my son has chosen to marry?' she enquired frostily. 'Pray come and sit down.'

She obeyed; her legs felt so weak that she almost collapsed into the chair opposite her inquisitor—a low armchair that placed her at several inches' disadvantage. Beneath that disapproving scrutiny she could feel herself squirm.

'Well—I had wondered why Daniel chose to leave it to the newspapers to inform me of the event,' Lady Amory remarked with nice distaste. 'I think the reason now becomes clear.'

Rae felt herself bridling. It was understandable that Daniel's mother would be upset, but there was no need for her to be so rude! 'I'm afraid Daniel was called away last night,' she responded, trying to be equally cool. 'Otherwise he would have been in touch with you to explain.'

'Explain?' One fine eyebrow lifted a fraction of an inch. 'Yes, it would seem that an explanation would be in order. So far as I was aware, when he went out to the Far East he was simply going on a business trip. I had no idea that he intended anything else.'

'He didn't—we didn't even meet until the night before we came home.'

Lady Amory looked slightly shocked. 'Do you mean to tell me that he married you the day after he met you?' she demanded.

'Yes. You see——'

'Lythgoe, I think I need one of my tablets,' the grand lady demanded in carefully measured distress, turning to a grey-suited gentleman whom Rae hadn't even noticed before.

'Of course, Lady Amory.' He hurried across the room to pick up her handbag, which was on the floor at her feet, and place it in her hands with solicitous care. 'Please try not to upset yourself.'

She seemed in little danger of withering as she snapped open the bag and took out a tiny mother-of-pearl pillbox. She slipped one pill into her mouth, and reached for the glass of brandy at her side, before fixing Rae with that acid glare again.

'And how *did* you meet?' she enquired, as if she could hardly bear to hear the answer.

But Rae's sympathy had not been engaged by that selfish little performance, and it seemed that she had already been judged and found severely wanting anyway, so she might as well give the old trout the unvarnished truth.

'I was working in a night-club,' she explained bluntly. 'I'm a dancer. Daniel came in, and after he'd bought me a couple of drinks we decided to leave together. Anyway, I was having a little trouble with the police, and I wanted to get out of the country as quickly as I could, so Daniel offered to help me.' All right, it was *very* unvarnished, but why bother with explanations that wouldn't be believed?

'So you persuaded him to marry you?' queried Lady Amory, aghast.

'No; actually he persuaded me. I wasn't particularly keen on getting married—it could interfere with my career. But... well, it seemed like a good idea at the time.' She shrugged her slim shoulders. 'At least it convinced the police to lay off me.'

'I see.' It was clearly costing considerable effort for Daniel's mother to control her horror at the story that was unfolding. 'And what do you propose to do now?'

'Do? I dunno.' She was overacting outrageously, but her audience was clearly ready to believe the very worst of her. 'I might stick around for a while, I suppose. Danny ain't short of a bob or two.'

Sharp eyes, almost as dark as Daniel's, regarded her with aristocratic disdain. 'Do you seriously suppose that this marriage has the least chance of succeeding?' she enquired coldly.

Rae lounged back in her chair, crossing her legs. 'I'm not really bothered,' she responded with another dismissive shrug.

'But you're hoping that when it fails, my son will be obliged to furnish you with a comfortable meal ticket? I'm sorry, young woman, but this is not

California—I think you'll find you have seriously misjudged the temper of the British divorce courts. And possibly that you have seriously misjudged Daniel. He's no fool.'

'He married me,' Rae couldn't resist pointing out.

'Quite. No doubt as an act of misguided chivalry, to assist you to leave the country you were so anxious to escape. But if you think you will be able to squeeze any money out of him, I'm afraid you're very much mistaken.'

'Am I?' Rae was almost shaking with suppressed rage, but she met the old lady's glare in defiant challenge. 'We'll see.'

One narrow white hand clenched on the arm of the chair, but Lady Amory forced a thin smile. 'You may take that chance. On the other hand, you may prefer to consider an offer I am prepared to make to you.'

'Oh?'

'Since you say that you don't particularly care about this marriage, I am willing to offer you five thousand pounds to make a statement that will allow Daniel to have it annulled.'

It was all Rae could do to control the cold fury that was rising inside her. She itched to tip this obnoxious woman backwards off her chair. But a smart little voice in her brain suggested a better way of getting revenge. 'Five thousand?' she drawled with lazy indifference. 'Is that all?'

'How much would you consider?'

'Well . . . If I sold the story to the papers, they'd probably offer me at least twice that.'

'Very well, ten thousand,' Lady Amory conceded tautly.

'On the other hand,' Rae mused, pretending to give the matter careful consideration, 'it could be rather fun to get my picture in the papers. It certainly wouldn't do my career any harm to get a bit of publicity——'

'How much do you want?'

'Twenty thousand.' She would *never* swallow that!

'Twenty thousand? Lythgoe—the briefcase.'

'But my dear Lady Amory——'

'I have the money here in my briefcase—in cash,' Lady Amory informed Rae, her voice sharp with contempt. 'My solicitor here has drawn up an affidavit that will adequately cover the situation. Also an agreement that precludes you from selling your cheap little story to the newspapers.'

Rae was fairly sure that such a contract could not be legally enforceable, but she kept such shrewd thoughts to herself. 'OK, you're on,' she agreed cheerfully. 'Give us the what's-its-name thing, then.'

Lady Amory opened the briefcase, careful not to allow her the opportunity to glimpse what was inside—just how much money had she brought with her to buy off her son's wife? She took out a sheaf of papers, which she handed to Rae

'Got a pen?' Mr Lythgoe passed her his own, and Rae scrawled her signature on the bottom of the sheets, barely bothering to read them through.

After all, this was exactly what she had wanted, wasn't it? A swift annulment—and now she wouldn't even have to see Daniel to arrange it. In fact, once his mother had described this little scene to him, he was never likely to want to see her again. Which neatly solved all her problems in one fell swoop. 'There you are,' she declared breezily. 'Well, let's see the money, then.'

Lady Amory eyed her with profound dislike. 'Each of these contains one thousand pounds,' she informed her in glacial tones, as one by one she laid out twenty packets on to the table beside her chair. 'Do you wish to count it?'

Rae reached for one pack, and swiftly checked it—it contained twenty crisp fifty-pound notes. 'That'll do,' she conceded, handing over the affidavit. 'Well, thank you. It was very nice doing business with you.'

'The agreement includes a clause that you should leave this house at once,' Lady Amory insisted.

'All right. It won't take me long to get my stuff.' She rose to her feet, and picked up the money. 'Cheerio, then,' she added saucily. 'See you around... Well, no, maybe not.'

She made her escape from the room before her mask of insolent indifference should slip, and raced up the stairs to where Mel was hovering anxiously on the landing.

'What happened...? My God, Rae, where did you get all that money?' she gasped.

'It's a long story.' She stepped past her friend into the bedroom she had shared with Daniel, and dumped the money on the bed. 'Have you got your things packed? We're leaving right now.' She dragged her bag up on to the bed, and began to stuff her clothes into it with more haste than care.

'But, Rae...there's thousands of pounds here,' Mel breathed, kneeling on the floor and picking up one of the packets almost reverently.

'Twenty thousand, to be precise. Daniel's mother gave it to me in return for a promise to get out of her son's life for good.'

'What?' Mel blinked up at her, confused. 'But...I don't understand. Why would she give you all that money?'

'Why indeed?' returned Rae bitterly. 'Don't worry yourself about her—she's obviously got far more of it than is good for her, and she thinks it gives her the right to go around insulting anyone who hasn't got any.'

'But... Well, at least it solves one problem,' declared Mel brightly. 'You've more than enough here to get a really nice flat. In fact you could almost afford to buy one—or at least put down a fat deposit.'

'Oh, no, I couldn't,' countered Rae, her mouth tight. 'I'm not keeping a penny of it.'

Mel stared at her in horror, instinctively reaching to protect the precious bundles. 'You're not going to give it back?' she pleaded.

'No. I'm going to give the lot to Oxfam.'

The music was a selection from *Gigi* and some of the other famous shows. The audience would be surprised, Rae reflected wryly as she moved gracefully through the well-rehearsed steps, to have known that most of the dancers in this typically Parisian review were actually English.

At least Les Oiseaux was a considerable improvement on the last place they had worked! Just off the Champs Élysées, it was not quite as saucy as the Moulin Rouge or the Crazy Horse, but it tended to be very popular with the tourists.

They had been lucky to get this job; not only had it offered the prospects of regular wages and a place to live, neither of which had seemed very forthcoming in London, but it had taken Rae well away from London—which had seemed like an excellent idea at the time.

It had been almost two months now. At first she had been terrified that Daniel would come after her. The story had been the toast of the Sunday papers for several weeks—'The Banker and the Bimbo'. They had twisted it all so cleverly, making that one brief and angry phone-call sound like a full-scale interview, and printing that snatched photo as if she had posed for it. And they had really slavered over the details of the Paradise club.

Three young men at a table in the front row were gazing up at her in hungry admiration, and she flashed them a meaningless smile across the footlights. This was just her job, to dance up here in a silver-spangled tailcoat that moulded her slender figure like a glove, and fishnet tights and high heels that made her legs look as if they went on for ever. If silly boys chose to weave their erotic fantasies about her, that was up to them—so long as they didn't try to come near her.

... Two-three-four *turn* and dip and doff her silver top hat ... She blinked in surprise as Mel leaned close to her. Whispering on-stage was definitely not allowed—Madame Lulu would be furious if she caught her.

'Rae—he's here!'

'*What...?*' She almost lost her balance. 'Where?'

'Table at the front, just to the left of the stage.' She indicated with a slight nod of her head. 'I'm sure it's him. I thought I saw him a while ago, further up the back, but he's just had the waiter bring him down closer.'

Rae's heart had begun to flutter in panic. This was what she had been afraid of. Every single night she had been on tenterhooks all the time she was on stage, afraid that Daniel would come in—but after all this time she had finally begun to think that she was safe.

It was certainly no coincidence that he was here. This was not the sort of place he would casually frequent, even if he happened to be in Paris on business—it wouldn't be sophisticated enough for his tastes. She tried to squint her eyes to look over the footlights as she moved back across the stage.

Was it him? There was certainly a man sitting there, on his own. She could just make out a pair of wide shoulders, moulded by a well-tailored dark jacket, and a hand resting on the white tablecloth, beside a vase of rosebuds. But she couldn't see his face—it was hidden in the shadows. The tiny hairs on the back of her neck began to prickle. *Was* it him?

So intent was she on trying to see that she almost missed the cue in the music, and had to retreat in double-time to get off the stage at the right moment. From behind the wing-curtains she peered out cautiously. Now the footlights weren't in her eyes, and she could see. It was him.

'Now, now, Raeleen—why is it that I must always scold?' Madame Lulu—seventy, if she was a day, but still vivacious—came up behind her, startling her. 'You gossip on the stage, and make the mistake, and now you must be peeping through the curtains to see the handsome man in the audience, instead of making ready. He must be very nice, to cause all this trouble, hm?' She tweaked the curtain aside, and glanced out, following the direction that Rae had been looking. 'Ah, yes!' she approved, her voice redolent of many memories. 'It is understandable, perhaps? I thought that such men had all disappeared!' She chuckled with laughter, but then at once she was businesslike again. 'But come—there is no time for moon-dreaming during the show. Hurry—it is your Apache dance next, no?'

'Oh, please, Madame Lulu, I...I think I've sprained my ankle,' Rae gasped desperately.

Bright button eyes regarded her in frank scorn. 'What is this? Show me,' she insisted sharply.

With a sinking heart, Rae lifted her foot, and Madame Lulu ran her tiny hands over her ankle, expertly diagnosing that there was absolutely nothing wrong.

'Tsk! No more of this nonsense now. Go, get into your costume. He has come to see you dance, has he not? Then dance for him!'

Rae felt her mouth uncomfortably dry as the stab of the spotlight caught her. Unconsciously she ran her tongue over her lips, and a rippling breath ran round the audience—they had thought it was part of the act.

She must look every inch the cheap bargirl in this costume, she reflected wryly. Her black satin skirt was slit to the thigh, and the striped leotard-top clung intimately to every curve of her body. The music played, and she sashayed across the stage, her high stiletto heels making her hips sway provocatively. She knew that every eye in the place was riveted on her.

At the side of the stage had been set a bar, with two customers in high-collared trenchcoats and low trilby hats—to disguise the fact that they were actually spare girls from the troupe—who were pretending to drink glasses of Pernod.

Rae leaned her elbows back on the bar, curving her body so that the firm swell of her breasts strained against the tight fabric of her top, and invited one of the 'men' to light the cigarette in the long holder dangling from her scarlet-tipped fingers.

This dance had never bothered her before—it was just a rather good, gymnastic piece, demanding a lot of the dancer, and she had rather enjoyed the acting that was an essential part of it. But tonight she felt...uncomfortable, exposed. He was out there watching her. What was he thinking? Why was he here? Had he at last come to take his revenge?

The drums rolled dramatically, and Paul—her male partner—appeared on the far side of the stage. He spent two hours every day working out with weights to develop that superb musculature, and even though she had seen him only this afternoon sitting crosslegged on the floor, his face puckered in short-sighted concentration as he darned a hole in his leg-warmers, she had to admit that he looked every inch the part now—mean, moody and magnificent.

There were audible gasps from the audience as he strode across to the bar and grabbed her by the wrist, pulling her against him. She braced her hands against his shoulders, her body a perfect arc, her eyes flashing dangerously, challenging him in defiance even as he swung her round with every appearance of rough anger, and flung her across the stage.

She tossed back her hair, the suppleness and grace of her body almost feline as Paul lifted her. The music was the theme from *Maigret*, very atmospheric, and she was losing herself in the dance—though now and again, from the corner of her eye, she could catch a glimpse of that dark, unmoving figure just beyond the footlights. And the fear she had to display in the performance was mirrored in her heart.

As they came to the final part of the routine, Paul threw her once more to the floor, and moved across the stage to lounge at a table upstage, where a pretty waitress—Mel, typecast—came to flirt with him. Slowly Rae rose to her feet, and reached over to the bar.

The ending was classic; the gunshots, the heart-broken remorse, the police arriving to drag her away in handcuffs—it was a scene that must have been acted out in dozens of stage shows all over Paris since the dance had first been choreographed.

The audience loved it, applauding loudly, and Rae had to force a smile as she stood with the others to take her bow. But her mind was in a panic. He was still there, almost menacing in his stillness. The show was almost over—just one more change now for the finale. And then what? Would he come after her? If he had managed to find her in Paris, where could she hide next?

# CHAPTER SEVEN

'RAE, are you all right?' asked Mel anxiously. 'You don't think he's going to come backstage or anything, do you?'

'Who knows what he might do? I don't even know why he's here... Damn!' Her hands were shaking so much that she was having difficulty pinning her hair up with the tortoiseshell comb that would hold it in place for the finale—the cancan.

'Here, I'll do that for you,' offered Tracy; one of the other dancers, she had been with the troupe for over a year, and often complained that she went through the many costume-changes in her sleep.

Rae regarded her own reflection in the mirror. The red satin and black lace of the dress should have clashed appallingly with her auburn hair, but somehow it seemed to enhance its glowing richness instead. The tight basque cinched her tiny waist and scooped up her breasts invitingly, emphasising their soft roundness... Biting her lip, she tried to ease the cups up a little higher, brushing up the ruffles around the top and lifting them high on her shoulders to conceal as much as she could, but it still seemed far too provocative.

'Do you think he knows where you live?' Mel went on. 'What if he comes round?'

'That's what I'm afraid of,' Rae confessed, dry-mouthed. 'If he could find out where I'm working...'

'Why don't you stay at my place tonight?' offered Tracy generously.

'Oh...I couldn't,' Rae demurred. 'I wouldn't want to put you to any trouble...'

'It wouldn't be any trouble,' Tracy insisted. 'I'll get Louis to run you over there after the show. I know just how you feel—there's nothing worse than a man who doesn't know how to take no for an answer.'

'But where will you stay?'

Tracy laughed, the throaty laugh that brought her more gifts of flowers and perfume, and many presents much more expensive, than any other girl in the troupe. 'He can come back here and pick me up—I fancy going out to St Cloud for breakfast.'

Madame Lulu bustled in, clapping her hands. 'Come along, girls, make haste. It is time for your entrance. Melissa, my child, you have on only one earring. Swiftly, swiftly, find the other. Raeleen...'

She tipped her bird-like head on one side, regarding Rae's appearance with a critical eye, and then with a decisive movement she eased the ruffles back down off her shoulders, revealing a deeper glimpse of the tempting shadow between her breasts.

'There! And *smile*, my little one. The cancan must be danced with all the wicked fun of the naughty nineties, you understand? Otherwise it will not work. Hide what you are feeling inside, and enjoy yourself.'

Rae had to run to catch up with the others, and arrived on the tiny oval stage already a little breathless. The music was instantly recognisable, and the audience had caught the excitement—this was what they had come to Paris to see, as French as snails in garlic and the Eiffel Tower.

With a whoop she cartwheeled across the stage, flashing a first tantalising glimpse of the black stockings and suspenders she wore beneath her ruffled skirt, and even of her frilly scarlet satin knickers. All around her the other girls were whirling and spinning in a dizzying kaleidoscope of bright satin and lacy frills—only Madame Lulu's insistence on endless rehearsals enabled them to pack the tiny stage without crashing into each other.

She danced down to the front, half blinded by the footlights, and, lifting her skirt, she twirled her foot, kicking her leg high, smiling flirtatiously at the sea of faces, anonymous faces, in front of her, teasing them with another saucy flash of her frilly knickers.

She had checked, and he was still out there, watching her, half hidden in the shadows—she could feel the heat of Daniel's unseen gaze resting on her. And, though there were probably a hundred people in the audience, she was aware only of him. Her body seemed to be responding as if he had touched her, her breasts tingling, her thighs aching with hunger. A kind of wanton recklessness had caught her, and she flaunted herself with a shameless abandon, challenging him to despise her.

With the others she fell into line and turned her back as they bent over and tipped their skirts up over their heads so that the audience was treated to the sight of a dozen pairs of long legs in stockings and suspenders, and a dozen pert *derrières* wiggling in their satin knickers. Then the line broke in the middle, and they skipped down to the footlights in pairs, throwing up their skirts again and kicking up their legs, promising far, far more than they intended to deliver.

What was he thinking as he sat there, so still? Was he remembering, as she was, how he had held her slender body in his arms, how he had gazed at the ripe naked swell of her breasts, caressed them, felt the tender nipples hardening into his palm? Now, as she lifted her skirt, was he imagining himself stroking his hand up over her slim, smooth thighs . . . ?

She had known that he would come after her, sooner or later. He had delayed long enough to show his contempt, but he would take his revenge. She had cheated him. It was more than just the money—she had caused his name to be dragged through the dirt. He was bound to think she had deliberately sold the story to the newspapers, after promising that she would not. He would never forgive her for that.

She threw herself into the dance, breathless and light-headed, squealing excitedly as she turned more cartwheels, her skirts flying, her eyes bright. The audience was cheering and clapping along to the buoyant music, whipping themselves up to fever pitch as the performance keyed up to its final crescendo, and the line of girls threw up their skirts a last time, and one by one along the line went down into the splits.

The audience went wild, rising to their feet, stamping and whistling. Rae lifted her head, the tight basque an uncomfortable constraint around her breasts as she struggled to catch her breath. The table to the left of the stage was empty—Daniel had gone. All that remained was a pile of bruised petals, stripped from the rosebuds in the vase.

'Bye-bye. See you tomorrow—and thank you.' Rae waved at Tracy as she stepped into the passenger-seat of the low-slung scarlet sportscar. Tracy's boyfriend flickered her a wry smile, and gunned the engine. 'It's very kind of you to give me a lift,' she murmured.

'Ah, it is no trouble,' he assured her airily. 'It will take no more than a moment.'

The way he was driving it certainly wouldn't, Rae reflected as she gripped the edge of the seat. He had swung out into the traffic, causing a taxi behind them to swerve and blast its horn, and with a very rude Gallic hand signal out of the window he roared away.

Rae turned to look out of the back window to try to see if there were any cars following them, but as they turned into the Champs Élysées there were so many lights to dazzle her that she couldn't be sure. They crossed the Seine, and passed below the soaring lattice of the Eiffel Tower, and then turned into one of the quieter side-streets, where plane trees shadowed the pavements and the houses wore an exclusive air.

The rents here must be far too high for a mere cabaret dancer to afford unaided, Rae reflected wryly—but that was Tracy's business. The boyfriend drew the car to a halt at the kerb and Rae slipped out with another quick thank you, and hurried to let herself in through the front door.

It was pleasant to find herself in the luxurious first-floor apartment, instead of the damp, smelly boarding-house where most of the girls in the troupe were staying. There she and Mel had to share a room with two other girls, and baths were strictly rationed by the fierce dragon of a concierge.

The bathroom here was a confection of peach-coloured marble and frills. As she peeled off her clothes and wrapped her hair up in a fluffy white towel she ran a deep swirl of hot water, and laced it generously with some of Tracy's expensive bath-oil. Then she stepped into it, and sank down slowly into the soft, caressing warmth, closing her eyes.

At once the compelling image of Daniel's hard-boned face drifted into her mind, and a small shiver ran through her as she remembered the way he had sat there, so close, separated only by the dazzle of the footlights. She had escaped him tonight, but she didn't imagine that he would give up.

And when he found her...? There her imagination was inclined to wander way off course, drifting into realms that were pure fantasy. Memories of the brief time they had been together swirled in her brain, of the way he had kissed her, caressed her... A low moan broke from her lips, and she sank down lower into the warm water, her own hands stroking down over her slippery skin as the fevered images possessed her...

The sharp ring of the doorbell cut across her dreamy thoughts. Tracy, she thought at once, rising quickly out of the bath. Had she forgotten something? Or was it maybe one of her other boyfriends, hopeful of finding her alone? If it was, he would be disappointed. She wrapped herself in Tracy's green and white silk kimono, and padded out to open the door.

The light in the hall dazzled her for a split second, but as she saw the tall, wide-shouldered silhouette standing on the threshold she gasped, and tried to slam the door shut again. But he was too quick for her, banging it open and stepping inside, forcing her to fall back.

'Well, well.' Daniel closed the door behind him, driving her another few paces back down the hall. 'Nice place you've got here. I'm glad to see my mother's money was well spent.'

'Wh-what are you doing here?' she demanded breathlessly, too stunned to explain that it wasn't her apartment at all.

He let his eyes drift down over her in lazy contempt. 'Didn't you expect to see me?' he taunted. 'I saw your boyfriend in his flash car, bringing you home. I expected him to stay—why did you send him away?'

'You—you followed me?'

'Well, since you've moved from that dump my private detective first saw you in ... Oh, yes, I had a private detective on you,' he added as her eyes widened in shock. 'You were very wise to clear out of England as quickly as you did, my beguiling little witch. But you surely didn't think I was going to let you get away with it?'

She had retreated as far as she could go—now she was trapped in the corner where the hallway turned. She stared up at him, her heart fluttering with fear as she recognised that there was no trace of gentleness, of mercy, in that ruthless face. 'Why did you take so long?' she whispered, knowing that her fate was inescapable.

He laughed cruelly. 'If I'd come after you straight away, I don't think I could have been responsible for my actions,' he grated. 'And while it might have given me a great deal of satisfaction to break every bone in your body I had no wish to serve a long prison sentence on your behalf. You've done enough damage.'

'I ... I'm sorry...' she whispered.

'Sorry? Why should you be? The publicity surrounding our brief marriage doesn't seem to have done your career any harm.' He flickered another disparaging glance around the apartment. 'But then I suppose in your line of business any publicity is good publicity, the more sordid the better.'

She hung her head. It was far too late to even begin to try to convince him of her innocence now—he was too angry to listen.

He put his hand under her chin, forcing her head up so that she had to look him in the eye. 'Just tell me one thing,' he demanded fiercely. 'Did you plan it all from the beginning? Did you have me marked down as a sucker from the moment I walked into the room?'

'You're not going to believe me whatever I say——'

'Too right! You're nothing but a scheming, conniving little bitch! Twenty thousand—ye gods! If I'd had my way, you wouldn't have got a penny—but, if you didn't see me as a soft touch, you certainly saw my mother coming.'

She almost laughed at that. The idea of his formidable mother as a soft touch! But this was no moment to laugh. The savage anger in his eyes warned her that he was every bit as dangerous as she had feared.

'Oh, you played it all so cleverly,' he sneered. 'There you were, pretending so prettily that an annulment was exactly what you wanted, that the last thing on your mind was to take me to the cleaners for my reckless act of chivalry in rescuing you from the police... You know, I wouldn't mind betting you really did steal that money from the gorilla.'

'I didn't!'

'But what makes me really angry,' he snarled, his fingers sliding down to her throat and curling around it, 'was the way you promised my mother that you wouldn't sell the story to the papers, and then went right out and did exactly that!' His grip tightened, and he began to squeeze. 'That picture of you on the front page, posing so provocatively outside my door, that luscious mouth pouting...'

'Please...' He was beginning to strangle her, and suddenly she was terrified. She put up her hands to try to pull his fingers away from her throat.

'Oh, I'm not going to kill you—though that's what you deserve.' He was still holding her trapped against the wall, but his grip hadn't tightened any more. 'I just came to look at you, to see you for what you really are. To rid myself once and for all of the images that have been taunting me. For the first and last time I let my baser urges interfere with my judgement—well, that's a mistake I won't make again!'

She stared up at him, startled by his admission that he had been troubled by images of her.

He laughed again, menacingly soft. 'Oh, yes, you still have the same effect on me,' he confirmed, his voice rough. 'That doesn't surprise me. No other woman has ever had that kind of instant impact. I should have taken you when I had the chance, instead of being so damned chivalrous. At least then I wouldn't have had to cope with the distraction of always wondering what it would have been like.'

His eyes had darkened, and a new kind of panic stirred inside her. What was he going to do?

'And then I saw you up there on that stage,' he growled, moving in closer to her. 'The way you were dancing, with all those men watching you, all wanting to touch you... You're nothing but a cheap little tramp—and if I had any sense I'd walk away from here right now, before I do something I might regret...'

With his free hand he tugged loose the tie of the kimono, and it fell open. A dark flame flickered in his eyes as he subjected her body to a slow, insolent survey; every naked curve. She shivered in fear; there was no trace of gentleness, of mercy in that ruthless face. But she was trapped, unable to escape, unable to even cover herself... and as he laughed in mocking triumph she knew that the tender pink of her nipples had tautened to ripe buds, pert and inviting, betraying the humiliating fact that she couldn't control her response to him.

'I watched you dancing...' His voice was now husky in his throat, his breathing impeded. 'That tight-boned corset thing... I just wanted to throw you down and tear it off you, to taste the sweetness of your naked body, to caress your beautiful skin...' His hand slid up slowly from her midriff to mould the aching swell of her breast. 'It's like silk...so smooth, so perfect...' His thumb brushed across the exquisitely sensitised peak of her nipple, and she moaned softly. 'Your breasts are like firm peaches, your nipples like hazelnuts—or strawberries, ripe enough to eat.'

He bent his head, and drew one taut bud into his mouth, nibbling it and suckling at it, drawing a sob of sheer ecstasy from her.

'I wanted to run my hand up between those smooth, slender thighs...' As he matched the action to the words her eyes flew open in shock, to meet the fierce demand in his. 'Feel them yield beneath me, lose myself in the sweet, moist velvet heart of you...'

'No!'

'Yes...'

She couldn't help it—as he crushed her back against the wall, and she felt the intrusive touch of his fingers, seeking the most intimate caresses, a soft sigh escaped her lips, and she closed her eyes, surrendering to the warm tide of feminine submissiveness that was flooding through her.

She could feel the hard demand of a fierce male arousal, warning her that he would not wait, and suddenly she realised that he was going to take her right there against the wall. There was no time even to panic—she gasped in shock as he thrust into her with a power that would have overcome any resistance. But her supple dancer's body yielded to him without a check, so that there was nothing to warn him of her inexperience; maybe he wouldn't have even noticed—he was taking his pleasure with an intensity that could pay no heed to anything else.

She could only cling to him, offering herself to the deep, primeval rhythm of his possession, bewildered by the wildness of the storm that was raging around her, inside her. His mouth had descended on hers in a punishing kiss, his tongue forcing her lips apart to invade deep into the sweet, defenceless valley of her mouth, swirling over every delicate membrane, firing her blood. She wanted this too, had wanted it from the first moment she had met him . . .

Her head tipped back, and she could hear the harsh drag of her own breathing, ragged and impeded, hear her own voice crying out in a strange, unearthly sound from the dawn of time, and her spine arched in one last tremor of ecstasy that left her lost and helpless, spinning in a mindless vortex of space, sliding down the wall to land in a crumpled heap at his feet.

As reality slowly began to filter back, she tried to ease away from him, but he laughed, a low, husky laugh full of meaning, and, catching her arm, he dragged her roughly to her feet. 'Oh, no—that isn't going to be nearly enough,' he growled. 'Fifty rupals, wasn't it, for the pleasure of your body for one night?' he taunted. 'I'm going to be expecting a very great deal for twenty thousand pounds.'

She tried to struggle, sobbing in anger and shame that she had yielded to him so easily when it meant so very little to him. 'Let me go,' she protested raggedly. 'I'll . . . I'll call the police . . .'

He laughed again, subduing with ease her attempts to break free. 'Oh, no,' he chided with chilling assurance. 'I don't think they'd help you much. You're still my wife—the annulment hasn't gone through yet. And this is Paris. I think the police would be inclined to sympathise with the wronged husband.'

Her numbed mind could barely comprehend what he was saying. The annulment hadn't gone through? 'But . . . Daniel, stop! We can't . . . If we——'

'If we make love, we won't be able to get the annulment?' he taunted. 'Oh, no, you aren't going to trap me that easily. You've signed the affidavit already.'

'But . . . now it isn't true any more,' she pleaded desperately.

'Truth? Lies? You don't know the difference,' he sneered unpleasantly. 'You persuaded my foolish mother to pay you a very large sum of money to tell, as she thought, a lie—which was in fact the truth. Well, now we've turned the truth into lies, and lies into the truth. Easy, wasn't it?'

'No . . . Daniel, please . . .'

'And now you can quit that so beguiling act of innocence, as if you were the purest young virgin in the world. You are what you are, and we both know it. So—where's the bedroom?'

She stared up at him, acid tears pricking her eyes. Even now, he didn't know. How could he not have realised? Was his hatred so fierce that it had blinded him even to that?

'Where?' he demanded, looming over her in threat.

She pointed, unable to speak.

'Go on, then.'

He pushed her roughly down the hall. Her hands were trembling as she obeyed, twisting the handle and opening the door. On the threshold she hesitated, her heart fluttering with nervous apprehension, though she knew that any sign of resistance would only make him more angry.

He glanced around, a sardonic smile curving his hard mouth as he took in the sheer hedonistic luxury of Tracy's bedroom—the huge four-poster bed, draped with yards and yards of white lace, the white lace that covered the walls and windows in extravagant swags, and flowed across every table and chair in the room.

'Well—you've really gone to town in here, haven't you?' he remarked drily.

She turned to face him, knowing that it was far too late to even try to make him understand. His eyes were hard as black diamonds as they surveyed her, and instinctively she drew the loose wrap around her naked body, a quiver of fear running through her.

With a sardonic smile he put up his hand and dragged off his tie, and unbuttoned his shirt, shrugging it back off his shoulders. The mingled tension of apprehension and excitement was knotting inside her as she watched, unable to tear her eyes from him. The movement of hard male muscles beneath smooth bronzed skin, the scatter of rough dark curls across his wide chest... Suddenly she felt weak and helpless all over again.

'Come here,' he commanded softly.

She went to him, trembling. But as he put up his hands to each side of her face, tilting it up to his, she realised that he was shaking too, and a dark fire burned in his eyes as he gazed down at her. 'God help me, Rae, I still want you,' he rasped huskily. 'I don't care what you are—I've never wanted a woman the way I want you.'

He bent his head, and his mouth met hers in a kiss of such gentle sensuality that her heart seemed to stop beating. This wasn't what she had been expecting, and it totally undermined any defences she might have had left. As he gathered her up in his arms she forgot everything but her own simmering desire, and the soft silk wrap slid from her shoulders to the floor.

His kiss was plundering into every sweet, secret corner of her mouth, leaving her nothing in reserve. Her body was melting into his arms, her naked breasts crushed against the hard wall of his chest, the sensitive buds of her nipples tender to the rasp of his rough hair.

His hot mouth began to trace a path over her fluttering eyelids, finding the racing pulse beneath her temple, and swirling into the delicate shell of her ear. A deep, honeyed warmth was flowing through her veins, reducing her to a state of mindless bliss. His hand had stroked up to caress her breast, his clever fingers teasing the ripe nipple with a skill that sent sparks of fire snapping through her brain.

With easy strength he lifted her off her feet, and carried her over to the bed, dropping her down on it and standing over her, surveying her nakedness with undisguised hunger, and his deep, rich chuckle set her nerve-fibres tingling.

'That first time was good,' he murmured, smiling in slow satisfaction. 'But the next time is going to be even better, and the time after that . . . I'm going to take you in every way there is, and when I've done that I'll invent a few more. And it's going to take a very long time.'

His hand moved to the buckle of his thick leather belt, and as he unfastened it she felt her heart thud, and unconsciously she ran the pink tip of her tongue over her lips to moisten them.

Dark flame leapt in his eyes. 'You little witch— you're the most tempting thing I ever saw.' He grasped her ankle and drew her towards him, climbing on to the bed, now as naked as she was. He spread his body over hers, crushing her beneath his weight, holding her wrists down on the pillow and spreading her thighs wide apart with his own.

'There ought to be a law against women like you,' he growled, breathing the perfume of her hair. 'How many other lovers have you driven to the brink of insanity, made them forget everything that was ever important to them, just for one night in your bed? Do you get a kick out of it, seeing how far you can drag a man down with your wicked spells?'

Stung with humiliation, she tried to utter some kind of protest, but he silenced her with a kiss of the sweetest possession, his tongue swirling languorously over the delicate inner membranes, his strong teeth nibbling sensuously at the soft fullness of her lower lip.

His caressing hands were stroking slowly over her body, savouring every slender curve, from the smooth swell of her hips, over the peach-smooth plain of her stomach, and up to mould the firm ripeness of her breasts. And she was lost, surrendering totally to his persuasive seduction; at that moment she would have agreed to anything he asked.

Her tender nipples were already exquisitely sensitised to his touch, and as he rolled them beneath his palms, and brushed them with his thumbs, she shivered in pure pleasure, her spine arching to curve her body towards him invitingly.

'You belong to me,' he growled, his eyes glittering with a fierce possessiveness as he gazed down at her. 'You're mine, and I'm never going to let you go.'

Some part of her mind knew that she ought to try somehow to bring some sanity back into this situation, but as his sensuous tongue began to explore the quivering responses he could arouse in the tiny hollow behind her ear, and then wandered on down the long, vulnerable curve of her throat, she knew that she was lost.

His clever hands were moulding and caressing the ripe mounds of her breasts as his kisses circled over them, and she heard her own breathing, ragged and impeded, as she waited in ever-tightening anticipation for him to reach the eager peaks. And then at last his mouth closed over one rosebud nipple, tasting its sweetness, and she cried out his name on a sobbing sigh, her hands curling into his crisp dark hair.

This was the most exquisite sensation she had ever known. He was suckling with a deep, hungry rhythm, his teeth scuffing her tender flesh, his lips pulling gently, driving her wild. He raised his head, laughing in soft triumph, but only long enough to turn his attention to the other nipple, treating that to the same searing desecration.

His possessive hand was caressing her with slow sensuality, stroking down the length of her spine and over the softly swelling curve of her derrière, and then further, down the silken length of her slender legs. And then as his hand smoothed back up, insistently parting her thighs, she quivered in vulnerability. But she could only yield, permitting him the most intimate caresses.

He knew exactly how to awake her responses. She whimpered softly, turning her face into the pillow as his seeking fingertips gently explored the soft folds of velvet, and found the tiny seed-pearl nestled within. She could hardly bear for him to touch it, so acute was her sensitivity, but when he did she was instantly flooded with such a warm tide of pleasure that she lay back, submissively allowing him to take any liberty he wished.

He was weaving a spell around her, binding her to him with the magic of his touch so that she would be his sexual slave for ever. His mouth was plundering her aching breasts, subjecting each tender nipple in turn to his sweet torment, and then moved on, exploring every inch of her burning skin, treating her to delights she would never have dreamed possible.

Her spine was curling in ecstasy; he was keeping his promise, making love to her in ways she would never have imagined, moving her to his will, and she submitted to everything he demanded, her body seeking only to please him. And some deep feminine instinct inside her taught her some inventive new ways of her own, and she caressed him with her hands and her lips, unsure at first but growing in confidence as the unmistakable tremors of his hard male response told her that he was enjoying what she was doing.

And then, just when she was sure that she must have reached the ultimate pinnacle, he took her again, and she found that there were heights to soar to beyond anything she had experienced so far. His powerful body dominated hers, thrusting into her with a driving rhythm that sent her spinning into a whirlpool of fire.

Time had no meaning for them—only sheer exhaustion could make them stop, but then within moments they were hungry for each other again. He would lie spread-eagled on his stomach as she massaged the smooth muscles in his back, thrilling to their power, bending her head to kiss the fascinating hollows in his shoulders where she had found a throbbing pulse, and then he would turn beneath her as she knelt over him, reaching up to caress her breasts, and she would toss back her hair, gasping with delight as he teased the tender pink nipples with his clever fingers.

And then he would span her slender waist with his hands, coaxing her to surrender to the full measure of his demand, and she would sway her hips in an erotic dance, like an odalisque pleasuring her master, until the tension inside him had gathered almost to the point of explosion, and he would throw her down on her back, buffeting her in a fierce tempest of passion until they were both consumed by the incandescent conflagration and were left like smouldering embers, finally sleeping.

'What on earth are you doing?' Rae had woken with a start, memories of the night rushing back as she sat up sharply. Daniel, now wearing his trousers but with his shirt still unfastened, had opened the doors of Tracy's capacious wardrobes, and was pulling out piles of clothes.

'Pack your things,' he ordered in that voice that would brook no argument. 'I'm taking you home with me.'

'*What* ...?' She scrambled off the bed, frantically trying to pick up Tracy's expensive dresses as he tossed them on the floor. 'Stop it—you'll ruin them,' she pleaded distractedly, trying to put them back on their hangers as quickly as he was adding to the pile.

'Leave them,' he rapped fiercely. 'I'll buy you as many dresses as you want. Just bring what you need for the journey.'

'Daniel, please,' she protested. 'I can't go back with you ...'

'You're my wife,' he grated, dragging her roughly into his arms. 'I want you where you belong.' His hot mouth burrowed into the sensitive hollow of her throat. 'I love you, Rae. I'm ready to sell my soul just to have you.'

'No!' Horrified at his words, she fought fiercely against the weakness that would have had her surrender and agree to whatever he demanded. She braced her hands against his shoulders, struggling to push him away. 'I am *not* your wife,' she insisted. 'Last night doesn't make any difference...'

He caught her arms in a vice-like grip, shaking her fiercely. 'You hard-faced little bitch,' he snarled, his eyes blazing with dark anger. 'How can you stand there and say a thing like that? I'm telling you I've fallen in love with you. Oh, it was the last thing I intended to do—I knew you were poison from the moment I met you. But you've won—poor insane fool that I am, I'll go down on my knees and beg you to come home with me if that's what you want.'

She stared up at him, stunned. It was the one thing she had longed to hear him say—that he loved her. But this wasn't the kind of love she wanted; this was a love so close to hatred that it was impossible to distinguish, a love born of nothing but sheer physical lust.

And within days he would know that, and would begin to despise the very sight of her. But at the moment no rational argument would make any sense to him. The only way to make him leave her was play the hard-bitten vixen he believed her to be, play it so convincingly that his anger would turn and drive him away from her—forever.

She shook her head, her face a mask of cool contempt. 'But I don't want to be married,' she asserted bluntly. 'It would be such a bore.'

He laughed with sardonic humour. 'A bore?
When you can have everything you've ever dreamed
of? You can go shopping every day—you can have
more pairs of shoes than Imelda Marcos.' He aimed
a disdainful kick at one of Tracy's strappy silver
sandals.

'I don't want to be a bird in a gilded cage,' she
countered. 'I have my career...'

His eyes glinted. 'You call that a career? Wiggling your bottom for every man who wants to ogle
at you?'

'It's better than wiggling it just for you!' she
flashed back. 'At least I'm independent—I can
come and go as I please, and I don't have to answer
to anyone.'

'No? And what will you do when the money you
got out of me runs out? Find some obliging
gentleman to pay the rent for you? Maybe I should
write out a testimonial for you—you'd certainly give
the poor sucker his money's worth, for as long as
it suited you.'

She gritted her teeth, forcing herself to swallow
the insult. The lower he thought her, the more surely
he would leave her alone. She picked up one of
Tracy's skimpier dresses—a sensational little
number in silver lamé—and concentrated all her attention on arranging its narrow straps back on the
hanger.

'I don't need your help,' she tossed at him in
casual indifference. 'I can take care of myself.'

'Well, I damned well hope you can,' he grated,
snatching up his jacket and tie. 'I was fool enough

to help you once, but I'll see you in hell before I ever lift a finger for you again.'

He slammed out of the flat, banging the front door with a force that reverberated through the whole building. Rae crumpled slowly to the floor, her eyes flooding with tears.

# CHAPTER EIGHT

'OK, PEOPLE, that's about it for today.' The dance-director clapped his hands. 'Thank you all for working so hard. I'll see you back here tomorrow morning, same time—and no excuses will do for lateness,' he added, slanting a meaningful look at Rae and Mel.

'Slave-driver,' muttered Mel, collapsing on the floor where she stood, and unfastening the tie of her pink ballet-shoe.

'Mmm.' Rae would have liked to have been able to sit down too, but she was in a hurry. 'I'll see you tonight, Mel. I've got to dash.'

Her friend squinted up at her in concern. 'You know, you're really overdoing it,' she warned. 'You look shattered.'

'I know, but I need the money,' Rae reminded her. 'If I can just do a few more of these videos . . . I won't get far on a waitress's pay, and besides I'll have to stop working altogether in another couple of months—the baby's due in April.' She turned sideways to examine her silhouette in the long practice-mirror. 'It doesn't show too much yet, does it?' she asked anxiously, patting the slight swell of her stomach.

'If you'd kept some of that money you got off Daniel's mother——'

'I wouldn't have touched a penny of that,' Rae declared fiercely. 'I don't want any help from the Amorys. I can manage by myself.'

Mel sighed. 'All right,' she conceded. 'I know better than to waste my breath. Though I do think you should at least tell him...'

'I don't suppose he'd want to know,' Rae insisted, a bitter note in her voice. 'Fathering a child on some cheap little dancer, whose name he probably can't even remember by now...?'

'Technically speaking,' Mel felt obliged to point out, 'you were actually married to him at the time, so the baby's going to be his legitimate child.'

'All the more reason not to tell him,' Rae responded briskly, picking up her kit-bag. 'I'm sure it's an episode he'd very much prefer to forget— and so would I!'

The November weather was miserable. Rae joined the long queue at the bus-stop, huddled under her umbrella, and when the bus finally came she had to stand most of the way. Just for one fleeting moment, she let herself dream of being swept away in the blissful comfort of a dark blue Rolls-Royce to a warm house in Belgravia, where a loving man would settle her with cushions, and insist she put her feet up...

But dreams were wasted—grim reality was struggling to make ends meet by holding down two jobs, and a damp attic flat that she would probably be kicked out of after she'd had the baby. Maybe she *ought* to tell Daniel—for the baby's sake, to give it at least some chance of a decent life...

But no—she would manage, somehow, just as her mother had managed. She had told her mother, of course—just the bare bones of the story, not the whole thing. Somehow she had made herself put a cheerful face on it, and though her mother had been upset at first she had been ready to accept that in this day and age it would be far less of a problem to be a single parent than it had been for her.

She didn't know what she would have done without Mel. That morning, after Daniel had gone, she had been distraught, not making any coherent sense. All she could say was that she never wanted to dance again. Mel hadn't even hesitated, throwing up her job too and coming back to England with her.

They had managed to find a flat, at exorbitant rent, and Rae had found a job as a waitress in a pretentious little restaurant in Wandsworth. It was Mel who had persuaded her to keep up her daily practice routine, even though she no longer wanted a dance career, arguing that it would be good for both her and the baby if she kept herself in the peak of fitness. And it had only been to return some of that support that she had gone along with Mel to the auditions to dance on a pop video.

When she had been offered a job too she had almost turned it down, but the money was too good to refuse. There had been three more videos since then—though it was hard work, racing from rehearsals to the restaurant, swapping her days off to fit in with shooting schedules.

She was already five minutes late as she jumped down from the bus and hurried along the busy pavement. Though the restaurant was on the wrong side of the river, a long way from the sophistication of the West End, it took itself very seriously, and the head waiter was not best pleased when she dashed in breathlessly through the back door.

'Late again, Miss Dillon?' he enquired loftily, glancing at his watch. 'You really must make more effort, you know—there are plenty of other girls who would be more than grateful for this job, if you're not.'

'Yes, if they don't mind starving to death on the wages you pay,' she muttered under her breath, but she forced herself to pin a suitably chastened smile in place. 'I'm awfully sorry, Mr Morris—the bus was late.'

'Hrmph! Well, hurry up and get ready. I don't know—the way you young girls dress these days,' he added, shaking his head as he regarded her red and yellow striped leg-warmers with refined aversion.

Rae quickly opened her bag and pulled out her uniform, freshly washed and ironed. 'I won't be a minute, Mr Morris,' she promised, slipping into the poky lavatory that was the only place for the waitresses to get changed.

Five minutes later, neat in her black dress, her hair pinned up beneath a dainty white cap, a white lace apron around her waist, she emerged into the kitchen. The first customers were already in, and she hurried to make sure her tables were ready for the evening.

It was a very smart place. The cuisine was French, and the décor was modelled on one of the smartest Parisian hotels, all lush green palms and bronzed mirrors. The white tablecloths were pristine, and not a fingermark was permitted on the silver cutlery. It did a good trade, and even though it was the middle of the week Rae was kept pretty busy, hurrying backwards and forwards between her row of tables and the kitchen, laden with plates and dishes.

By half-past nine her back was aching and her feet were killing her—she would have loved to have been able to just lie down and go to sleep. But at least it was unlikely that many more people would arrive now, and as customers gradually began to leave and she was able to clear off her tables she would be able to snatch a moment or two to take the weight off her feet.

She was taking an order for coffee when the chill from the door's opening behind her told her that some late customers had come in. 'Monsieur Maurice' hurried forward with his most welcoming smile, reserved for those his professional eye recognised as being important enough to be granted one of the best tables without the formality of a prior booking.

'Thank you—a table by the wall will do very nicely.'

Rae felt an odd little shiver run down her back. That voice was so familiar—she had heard it every night in her dreams. But it *couldn't* be—she must be imagining... Swiftly she glanced up into one of the bronzed mirrors, and those hard dark eyes met hers with not a trace of surprise. Then he turned away, smiling down at the willowy blonde at his side, inviting her to precede him through the restaurant.

'...with cream, please.'

She blinked, struggling to turn her attention back to the customers at the table. 'I...I'm sorry, what was that?'

'Two coffees, one black and one with cream.'

'Yes.' She dived for the haven of the kitchen, fighting for breath. Daniel had seated himself at one of *her* tables—quite deliberately. He had known she was working here—he must still have that private detective keeping an eye on her. But why was he here?

Cautiously she peered out through one of the circular portholes in the kitchen doors. He hadn't changed—but then she wouldn't have expected him to. Still that air of cool arrogance, that indefinable male power that he seemed to exude without any effort at all. And his dinner-partner was hanging on his every word.

Rae bit her lip, a surge of fierce jealousy ripping through her. This beautiful creature was exactly the sort of thoroughbred of whom Lady Amory would have approved—racehorse slim, with rich-girl ash blonde hair and a delicately boned aristocratic face

and a chic suit of olive-green silk that bore the unmistakable stamp of couture cut. She was leaning
across the table, saying something to Daniel over
the top of the menu, and her hand moved to touch
his in a gesture that was quite natural and
possessive...

'Come along, Raeleen, it isn't time for you to
stand about daydreaming yet,' bustled the head
waiter, coming in through the other half of the
swing doors. 'There are some customers at one of
your tables—go and take their order.'

'Yes, Mr Morris, I'm...just getting coffee for
table six.'

'Well, hurry up about it, then.'

'Yes, Mr Morris.' As she hurried through into
the kitchen, she stopped one of the other waitresses. 'Brenda, do me a favour?' she pleaded in a
whispered undertone. 'Serve my table eight for me?'

Brenda pouted. 'How can I?' she protested. 'I've
still got five tables on dessert.'

'I'll do some of those for you.'

'Then what's wrong with table eight?'

'Now, now, girls, you don't have time to stand
around gossiping,' scolded the head waiter, coming
out from the wine cellar.

'I'm sorry, Mr Morris,' piped Brenda, set on
making sure she didn't get the blame. 'Rae was
asking me to serve one of her tables.'

His eyebrows shot up in a show of indignation.
'What on earth for? You know the rules. You all
serve your own tables—I'm not having you

swapping and changing around to suit yourselves. Whatever would happen?'

Rae sighed, and, picking up the two coffees for table six, she went back into the restaurant.

Daniel glanced up as she approached, and she knew from the dark glint in his eyes that he had not failed to recognise her. But he didn't acknowledge her in any way. She took her pad and pen from her pocket, and pinned her politest smile in place— he wasn't the only one who could wear a mask.

'Are you ready to order now, sir?'

'Yes, I think so. Philippa?'

The elegant blonde smiled across at him, a smile of carefully considered charm. 'I think I'll have the crab terrine, darling. With ... yes, the *escalopes de veau*, and a Waldorf salad. Not too many calories!'

'And I'll have the same,' he concluded briefly. As Rae jotted down the order he was already ignoring her presence, turning back to his companion. 'No, if I were you I'd stay well away from anything with such a high gearing. With interest rates high, any fall in the market could leave you holding just so much junk ...'

Rae moved away, back to the kitchen. She had certainly been put in her place this evening; she was there only to serve, while he chatted with his beautiful girlfriend—she didn't even know if he'd been talking about cars or stocks and shares.

She gave the chef the order, and went out again to clear some of the empty tables, trying her best not to look in the direction of the couple at table eight. But she couldn't help seeing them. Everywhere the mirrors reflected them as they talked and laughed together—intimately, like lovers.

She could almost feel the pain biting into her heart, as if it were a knife that he was turning inch by inch. Somehow she managed to serve them with their starter, the perfect waitress, unnoticed by either of them. But oh, how she longed to tip the delicate pink terrine right into his lap—or the damned blonde's! Just don't treat me like this! she wanted to shout at him. You made love to me once—I'm carrying your baby.

There were few customers left in the restaurant now, and she managed to stay hidden in the kitchen for a while. One of the junior chefs gave her a smile of sympathy, and poured her a cup of coffee to keep her going, and she sipped it secretly, hiding it behind a tub of flour so that Mr Morris wouldn't see.

But he came barging in through the double doors, looking for her. 'There you are!' he exploded. 'The people at table eight finished their terrine five minutes ago—go and clear the plates, and take them their entrée.'

She nodded weakly. It was all she could do to force herself back into the restaurant—it was so hard to see him sitting there with someone else, and feel that aching longing inside her for just one fleeting smile. His hand was resting on the table, that strong, sensitive hand that had caressed her so sensuously, and as she stepped behind him to pick up his plate she could breathe that subtle male muskiness that was so exclusively his own.

The tears were almost blinding her as she turned back towards the kitchen, the dirty plates in her hands. All she heard was a sudden cry of 'Look out!' and then the swing door opened sharply, catching her full in the face. She fell backwards with a clatter of plates, catching her arm on a chair as she fell, and hitting her elbow painfully on the floor.

She was half stunned from the blow on her forehead. Dizzily she tried to sit up, only to find a pair of strong arms around her, supporting her. Mr Morris, who had been the one to barge open the door, was fuming.

'I'm so sorry, sir—these girls, they're so silly, they don't look where they're going. Please, sir, return to your table. She isn't hurt. I'll have someone else bring your entrée——'

'You damned fool—can't you see how shaken she is?' she heard Daniel demand angrily. 'It was your fault—you were the one not looking where you were going.'

She was in heaven. Even if it was only for a few moments, she could close her eyes and lie back in his arms...

'Oh, dear!' Brenda had come fussing up, delighted by the drama. 'Are you all right, Rae? You look ever so pale. It's really bad for her to fall, Mr Morris. She's pregnant, you know.'

There was a moment of stunned silence, and Rae opened her eyes cautiously to look up. Philippa was standing just behind Daniel's shoulder, her expression one of refined distaste. 'Daniel? There's no reason for us to get involved in this, is there?' she pleaded with a pure aristocratic horror of a public scene.

'I'm sorry, Philippa,' he said, his voice very firmly indicating that he had every intention of becoming involved.

Those finely drawn eyebrows rose in angry surprise, and she cast a searching look at Rae. 'I know who she is!' she declared, pointing an accusing finger. 'I thought I recognised her—her picture was in the papers a couple of months ago. She's your wife!'

Mr Morris's expression ran the gamut from anger to amazement. 'Your wife?' he gasped. 'But... I'm sorry, sir, I had no idea. Of course, I ... Brenda, don't just stand there, you silly girl—get a chair.'

But Daniel picked her up in his arms as if she weighed nothing at all. 'It's all right, I'll take her home,' he said. 'If someone could just fetch her things? Philippa, I'm very sorry about this——'

'Oh, don't mind me at all!' she spat furiously. 'I thought you must be out of your mind at the time. A waitress...!'

Rae knew she ought to protest, but she couldn't find the strength. Her head hurt, and all she wanted to do was stay here in Daniel's arms, for ever and ever. She was aware that he was carrying her towards the door, with Brenda running along beside him clutching her kit-bag. It was still raining, but his car was parked at the kerb, and he placed her in it carefully, leaning across her to fasten her seatbelt. He put her bag at her feet, and then came round to climb in behind the wheel.

The engine purred to life, and he pulled out, taking the right direction for her flat without needing to ask her where she lived. She slanted him a cautious glance from beneath her lashes. 'You've had that private detective following me again.' It was a statement, not a question.

'I arranged that he would give me a follow-up report every so often,' he responded, his voice calmly matter of fact. 'I wanted to be forewarned if you were likely to be up to something that might cause me trouble.'

'So why did you come to the restaurant tonight?'

He paused, his attention on filtering out into the main road, before replying. 'Let's just say that I was curious.'

'Why?'

'I wondered what you were doing, skivvying in a restaurant. I couldn't imagine your taking to hard work.'

Her eyes flashed at the taunting note in his voice. 'Well, now you know. I'm pregnant.'

'Whose is it?'

'Not yours,' she retorted in instinctive self-defence.

'Well, at least you're honest.' He laughed drily. 'Or have you already got some other poor sucker lined up to pay maintenance?'

'If I did, do you think I'd be "skivvying", as you put it?' she demanded. 'Look, you can just drop me here—I'll walk the rest of the way. I'm all right now.'

'You don't look it,' he responded without any sympathy. 'And whatever kind of bitch you are, I can't leave you to faint in the street on a filthy night like this.'

She turned her head away from him, her throat too choked with tears to retort. She was remembering the last words he had said to her—'I'll see you in hell before I ever lift a finger for you again.'

It wasn't far to the street where she lived. Maybe once—long ago—the tall houses had been gracious, but they had fallen on very hard times. Daniel didn't say a word as he pulled his elegant car into the kerb behind a doorless wreck leaning drunkenly on its two remaining wheels.

He came round to open the door for her before she could find her way out of her seatbelt. 'Thank you for the lift,' she managed, holding up her head with as much dignity as she could muster. 'Goodnight.'

'I'll see you up to your flat.'

'That won't be necessary...'

A flicker of that familiar sardonic smile crossed his face. 'I'm curious to see if it can really be as bad as the report described.'

She glared at him mutinously, but she knew better than to waste her breath arguing. In the tiny front garden, where only dandelions grew, a thin brown dog was rifling the contents of a fallen dustbin. The back-seat of the wrecked car had been dumped over the hedge, and was quietly rotting in the rain.

'What a charming neighbourhood,' he remarked with ironic humour.

'If you don't like it, don't stay,' she countered tartly. 'Get back to Belgravia, where you belong.'

She unlocked the front door, and kicked it sharply with her foot to free it from the warped frame. He followed her inside, pushing the door shut behind him, studying the unsavoury messages carved and painted on its back with mild interest.

'Careful,' she warned him grudgingly, leading the way up the steep, dark stairs. 'Don't trust the banisters.'

Actually she had to admit that she was glad of his support up the last flight—the stairs had never seemed like such a mountain as they did tonight, and he had relieved her of her heavy kit-bag too. At the top she paused on the ill-lit landing, and put her key into the door of her flat.

'Well,' she sighed wearily, 'here it is.'

It was as cold inside as it was out, and there was a damp musty smell that they could never quite get rid of, no matter what they did. To her relief there was a light on in the sitting-room, showing that Mel was home—she didn't want to be alone with him.

Unfortunately the living-room was as unprepossessing as the rest of the flat. They had painted over the ghastly wallpaper with a warm shade of burgundy, to try to make it seem a little more cosy, and they had filled it with plants. But the only thing the armchairs had in common with each other was that they were painfully shabby, in spite of the bravery of the bright scatter-cushions they had piled on them, and the posters on the walls did little to hide the dark patches of damp.

Mel was sitting on the floor to get as close as she could to the one bar of the electric fire that was working, watching the film on the black and white portable television, but she scrambled up as they came in, her mouth open in surprise. 'Rae...you're home early,' she managed lamely.

'Yes.' She turned to Daniel, her mouth tight. 'So—now you've seen it,' she said, waving her hand around the room. 'I'm quite sure it's every bit as bad as your sneak told you. Are you satisfied?'

He glanced around, a faintly sardonic smile curving his hard mouth. 'You really have come down in the world,' he remarked, a mocking note of sarcasm in his voice. 'What did you do with all the money you got from my mother? It didn't take you long to fritter it all away, did it?'

Rae didn't deign to answer. She walked across the room and sat down, grateful to be able to kick her shoes off, and leaned back with a yawn, shifting a cushion so that it comfortably supported the small of her back. Mel looked from her to Daniel, bemused.

'What's going on?' she asked. 'Rae, you've got a whopping great bump on your head.'

'I walked into a door.'

'Oh?' Mel eyed Daniel suspiciously, as if she thought he might have been the cause of the injury.

'I merely brought her home,' he explained, that glint of ironic humour lurking in his eyes.

'Oh. Well, I suppose that's the least you could do, under the circumstances.'

He lifted one sardonic eyebrow. 'I wasn't aware that the circumstances were anything to do with me,' he countered drily.

'Nothing to do with you?' Mel bristled with indignation on behalf of her friend. 'Well, it may interest you to know that she's pregnant.'

'I know that.'

Mel looked shocked. 'You mean you don't even care that she's carrying your baby?' she demanded fiercely.

Rae groaned. Trust Mel and her tactless tongue!

'*My* baby?' Daniel shook his head. 'I'm afraid you're mistaken—it isn't mine.'

'Well, who the hell else's do you think it could be?' Mel countered. 'You're the only man she's ever been to bed with.'

He laughed in cynical amusement. 'Oh, come on—I wasn't born yesterday——'

'I *know*,' retorted Mel, ignoring Rae's attempts to shut her up. 'I've known her since she was four years old—we went to the same nursery school, and we've been best friends ever since. I know how bad she felt about the way she had to grow up, with no dad. She learned a hard lesson from that—if there was ever anyone who wasn't going to fall for some smoothie who was just out for what he could get, it was her. Until she met you.'

'Mel . . .' protested Rae weakly.

'I'm sorry—I know I'm not very bright, and maybe I've got a big mouth, but there are some

things that have just got to be said. As if it wasn't
enough what his bloody snobby mother did,
treating you as if you were a bit of dirt... It just
makes my blood boil to see him standing there insulting you.'

She turned fiercely on Daniel again. 'If you don't
know a nice girl when you see one, I feel sorry for
you,' she berated him. 'You don't deserve her. Even
though she was crazily in love with you, she
wouldn't stay with you because of what people
might think, your associating with a dancer—as if
that would matter to anyone with a crumb of sense!
Well, I hope you're satisfied—you broke her heart.'

She stormed towards the door, but then turned
back. 'And I'll tell you one other thing, before I'm
finished,' she added as Rae picked up a large
cushion and tried to disappear behind it. 'You want
to know what she did with that dirty money your
mother gave her? She gave it to Oxfam—every
penny. She didn't even keep a single pound for
herself. So put that in your pipe and smoke it!'

The door slammed, and there was a long silence
in the room. At length Rae removed the cushion,
and risked opening her eyes. Daniel was standing,
his hands in his pockets, looking at her. 'I think
we'd better talk,' he said.

She nodded dumbly.

He moved over to sit down in one of the other
armchairs. 'Is it my baby?'

'Yes.'

His expression was unreadable. 'Why did you tell
me it wasn't?' he asked.

'Because... I don't want anything from you. I don't need you.' Tears were welling into her eyes, but she blinked them back. 'I can manage.'

'You call this managing?' He cast a disparaging eye around the room. 'For God's sake, Rae... At least you could have let me help you financially.'

'I wouldn't touch a penny of your money!'

She had spoken with a venom that seemed to take him aback. He shook his head, as if slightly bemused. 'All that money my mother gave you—you really gave it all away?'

'Yes,' she confirmed defiantly.

'But why? Why did you take it in the first place if you didn't want it?'

'Because she was so rude to me.' Rae screwed up her face at the memory. 'I'm sorry; I know she had every reason to be, but she made me so angry! She spoke to me as if I were nothing, assumed she could buy me off. I just decided to get as much money out of her as I possibly could... I suppose it was stupid, really, but at the time...'

He laughed wryly. 'I wish I'd been there to see it,' he remarked. 'I gather it was quite an act.'

'I'm sorry,' she mumbled, her eyes downcast.

'Oh, it served her right—as I told her at the time. She should never have tried to interfere, but she thought she was acting for the best. I'm afraid she can sometimes be rather silly and rather snobbish—but she isn't all bad, you know.'

She looked up at him, her eyes searching his face. 'You... aren't angry with me?' she questioned uncertainly.

'Tell me about the story in the newspapers.'

'I didn't sell it to them,' she told him earnestly. 'A reporter rang up, early in the morning the day after you went to Canada. I don't know how he'd got hold of the story, but he seemed to know most of it already, and I tried not to say anything, but somehow... He was twisting everything, tying me up in knots until I didn't know what I *was* saying.'

'That's how the gutter Press usually works,' he acknowledged, an inflexion of sardonic humour in his voice. 'And as for where they got the story from—I should imagine a certain Margot Havering in Kahyangan might be able to give us the answer to that one. She acts as a kind of unofficial correspondent in the area for one of the big news agencies, and she wouldn't be able to resist passing on a juicy titbit like that.'

'Oh... I never knew...'

'Why should you? I never told you.'

'In Paris... You said...'

'I said a lot of things that night in Paris that I didn't mean.' He came over to kneel beside her chair, enfolding her hands in his. 'That night...you were a virgin then, weren't you?' As she nodded, he demanded roughly, 'Why didn't you tell me, before I...?'

She flickered him a shy glance from beneath her lashes. 'You didn't seem as if you would have listened,' she whispered.

He groaned, and dropped his head into her lap. 'Oh, Rae—how could I ever have hurt you like that? I knew, and yet... I wouldn't let myself believe it.

Mel was right—I don't deserve you. Can you ever
forgive me?'

'Forgive you?' She couldn't help it—she just had
to stroke her hand over those crisp dark curls.
'There's nothing to forgive. It was my fault you
thought what you did—I'd given you every
reason——'

'No.' He lifted his head, and gazed up into her
eyes, his own as dark as drowning pools. 'I was a
fool—I should have trusted my instincts. Right from
the beginning, in spite of the way I met you in that
dump in Kahyangan, somehow I always felt inside
that you weren't what you seemed to be. You were
even worried about letting me buy you a few
clothes!'

She smiled, remembering that night so vividly. 'I
promised to pay you back, and I never did,' she
recalled.

He laughed softly. 'I was going to make you pay
me, at one time—every penny, even for the coffee
I'd bought you. I was planning to sue you. Fortunately Lythgoe talked me out of that one! It would
have looked very petty in court.'

'I couldn't imagine your ever doing anything
petty,' she asserted, smiling shyly.

'Oh, that was the least of what I wanted to do
to you!' His eyes glittered. 'It took my detective
less than a week to find out where you were. It
became like an obsession with me, plotting your
downfall—but somehow every scenario I planned
always ended with your lying on a bed with no
clothes on, begging me to make love to you.'

She felt her cheeks tinge with pink—things had turned out remarkably similar to the way he had planned!

'By the time I finally followed you to Paris, I thought I would be well able to keep myself under control. I had no intention of coming after you that night—I was just going to go into the club, and watch you from a distance. It was supposed to be some kind of final exorcism, to free myself of the dreams that had been haunting me ever since you left. But then I saw you, up there on that stage, and all I could think of was how much I wanted you. I would have torn down half of Paris to get to you. I waited outside, across the road, out of sight, until you came out, and when I saw you get into that red car... I could have murdered that guy.'

'It was Tracy's boyfriend,' she whispered. 'One of the other dancers. It was her apartment, too.'

He looked surprised. 'Not yours?'

She laughed, shaking her head. 'No—I could never have afforded a place like that, not on the money I was getting. She offered to let me stay there that night, because I was scared that you'd show up at the boarding-house we were living in.'

He let go his breath in a long sigh. 'It was that guy, and the sight of that flat... They were the last straw. I'd followed you in a taxi, and saw where you drew up, and I waited to see which light came on. I stood there outside, telling myself that you weren't worth it, that I should just walk away and forget all about you, but I could no more have done that than stop drawing breath. So I came up... and once I was close to you... I'm sorry, Rae—I wanted you so much...' His voice choked huskily.

'I wanted you too,' she confessed, her eyes resting on him in aching longing. 'I loved you.'

'Loved?' he repeated questioningly. 'Past tense?'

'I still love you.'

He took her hand, turning it over in his and placing one kiss on the fluttering pulse beneath her wrist. 'You're still my wife, Rae,' he told her, his voice not quite steady. 'I never went through with the annulment.'

She blinked at him in astonishment. 'Why not?'

'Because I didn't want to let you go. In Kahyangan... I could probably have thought of another way to get you away, you know, but when old George suggested I should marry you I knew that was exactly what I wanted to do. Oh, I admit I wasn't thinking very rationally at the time—all I knew was that I wanted to stake some sort of claim over you, write my name on you so everyone else would know to steer clear.'

'It was a lovely wedding,' she mused, smiling softly in reminiscence. 'I'll always remember that day, as long as I live. But... I can't be your wife, Daniel. You know that.'

His eyes flared. 'Why not?' he demanded roughly.

'It's impossible,' she insisted, a wistful sadness in her voice. 'You know that. I'm... I'm so unsuitable... Your mother...'

'I've no intention of allowing my mother to dictate to me whom I should or should not marry. Heaven knows she's tried to thrust enough "suitable" young ladies under my nose over the years. She's just going to have to get used to the fact that you're the one I've chosen. Give her a chance—I know she'll like you once she gets to know you.'

But still Rae shook her head. 'It isn't just your mother,' she insisted, determined to try and make him see sense. 'Oh, surely you must realise? Our backgrounds are so different—I won't fit in, your friends won't like me...'

He put his hands on each side of her face, and tilted it towards him. 'All I realise is that I love you,' he told her firmly. 'I don't give a damn about anyone else—anyway, anyone whose opinion I care about will judge you for themselves. Now will you stop arguing about it, and go and pack your things?'

'But...'

'Listen, Rae—I do see your point. I'm asking you to make a lot of changes, and I know it's not going to be easy for you. There's your career...'

She smiled wryly. 'Oh, I don't think I'd be a very great loss to the world of dance,' she confessed. 'I was never going to be much more than an average chorusline hoofer.'

'But if you want to carry on with it...'

She shook her head. 'No—maybe one day I'll teach it, like my mother did, but I don't want to go on the stage again. But that isn't the point—or at least, not all of it. Even if I've given it up, you can't want people saying you married an ex-dancer.'

'People can say what they damned well like. I'm not going to give you up, Rae. If you won't come home with me where you belong, I shall move in here!'

She began to laugh at that. 'No, you can't. Don't be silly...'

'Will you stop telling me what I can and can't do?' he demanded, a teasing glint in his eyes. 'I'm beginning to think I'm going to be a very hen-pecked husband.'

'Oh, no—never that,' she vowed quickly. She wrapped her arms tightly around his neck, all her objections laid aside. He was right—nothing else mattered except their love for each other. 'I'll never do anything to make you unhappy,' she promised. And as his mouth claimed hers she surrendered totally, losing herself in the world of his arms.

# BARBARY WHARF

**An exciting six-book series, one title per month
beginning in October, by bestselling author**

Set in the glamorous and fast-paced world of international
journalism, BARBARY WHARF will take you from the
*Sentinel*'s hectic newsroom to the most thrilling cities in the
world. You'll meet media tycoon Nick Caspian and his
adversary Gina Tyrrell, whose dramatic story of passion and
heartache develops throughout the six-book series.

In book one, BESIEGED (#1498), you'll also meet Hazel and
Piet. Hazel's always had a good word to say about everyone.
Well, almost. She just can't stand Piet Van Leyden, Nick's
chief architect and one of the most arrogant know-it-alls she's
ever met! As far as Hazel's concerned, Piet's a twentieth-
century warrior, and she's the one being besieged!

Don't miss the sparks in the first BARBARY WHARF
book, BESIEGED (#1498), available in October from
Harlequin Presents.

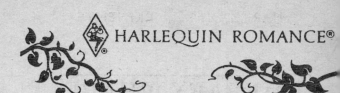

**HARLEQUIN ROMANCE®**

Harlequin Romance
knows love can be dangerous!

Don't miss
TO LOVE AND PROTECT (#3223)
by Kate Denton,
the October title in

# THE BRIDAL COLLECTION

**THE GROOM'S** life was in peril.
**THE BRIDE** was hired to help him.
**BUT THEIR WEDDING** was *more* than
a business arrangement!

Available this month in
The Bridal Collection
JACK OF HEARTS (#3218)
by Heather Allison

Wherever Harlequin books are sold.

# WELCOME TO

The quintessential small town, where everyone
knows everybody else!

Finally, books that capture the pleasure
of tuning in to your favorite TV show!

Join your friends at Tyler in the eighth book, BACHELOR'S PUZZLE by Ginger
Chambers, available in October.

*What do Tyler's librarian and a cosmopolitan architect have in common? What
does the coroner's office have to reveal?*

GREAT READING...GREAT SAVINGS...
AND A FABULOUS FREE GIFT!

Each book set in Tyler is a self-contained love story; together, the twelve novels
stitch the fabric of the community. You can't miss the Tyler books on the shelves
because the covers honor the old American tradition of quilting; each cover
depicts a patch of the large Tyler quilt!

And you can receive a FABULOUS GIFT, ABSOLUTELY FREE, by collecting
proofs-of-purchase found in each Tyler book, *and* use our Tyler coupons to save
on your next TYLER book purchase.

---